DIRT ANGEL

DIRT ANGEL

STORIES BY
JEANNE WILMOT

Ontario Review Press • Princeton

Ontario Review Press
9 Honey Brook Drive, Princeton, NJ 08540

Distributed by George Braziller, Inc.
171 Madison Avenue, New York, NY 10016

Library of Congress Cataloging-in-Publication Data

Wilmot, Jeanne.
Dirt angel : stories / Jeanne Wilmot. — 1st ed.
p. cm.
Contents: Dirt angel—Madonna—Red gables—Survivors—Spade in
the minstrel mask—The shopper—The tryst—The company we keep.
ISBN 0-86538-088-0 (cloth : alk. paper)
1. United States—Social life and customs—20th century—Fiction.
2. City and town life—United States—Fiction. I. Title.
PS3573.1456727D57 1997
813'.54—dc21   97-15303
                                              CIP

First Edition

Many of these stories have previously appeared
in the following publications:
"Dirt Angel" in *The North American Review*;
"Madonna" in *Antioch Review*; "Red Gables" in *Denver Quarterly*;
"Survivors" and "The Shopper" in *Ontario Review*;
"The Company We Keep" in *Antaeus*.
"Dirt Angel" was reprinted in *The O. Henry Awards*.
The title "Spade in the Minstrel Mask"
is taken from a screenplay by Frederick Dennis Greene.
Grateful acknowledgment is made
to the New York State Foundation for the Arts.

To my Mother and Father

and to my Grandmother

These stories would never have found their way into print without the ongoing support of Joyce Carol Oates. And it was Raymond Smith's editorial precision that shepherded this book to completion. To Jane Shapiro, my thanks for her tireless friendship and skill with the language. And special thanks to Daniel Halpern, whose editorial touch is present on every page.

CONTENTS

DIRT ANGEL

DIRT ANGEL

I T IS THE TIME OF YEAR THE GYPSIES come out of hibernation. The ochre-faced children make an altar of plastic roses when they see me heading up Broadway straight to Said's. I recognize the little ones who are new to the marketplace even though the willful charcoal eyes and the con are familiar. They learn to spit at grace young here. Immediately after returning from the hospital I changed into a red two-piece halter and shawl that match the first spring air. When I enter the club, Mario is holding court from his usual corner, speaking in chants that are in keeping with the cadence of his gang days, stabbing down into the air with his fingers, floating high on the hawk with the dust of an angel. I haven't been to Said's for a while. Haven't seen Mario for longer. Tonight I needed to be back home. I like my life now all right. I work a professional day job. I get up, have morning coffee and am at the hospital by nine. But this place, Mario, and the people here manage to sustain something close to the sense of silent commotion I associate with home—there is no routine, crisis is our energy and the silence is just the waiting for something to happen.

Mario glances at me quick as I rock into the center of the club, swivel-headed and a little coked up. A beautiful sandy-haired womanchild straddling a stool at the bar fixes on my small breasts. She looks as white as I look black, and for all her sexual smugness, I can smell the captive in her. Tall ferns and palms sway to a breeze propelled by a wind machine that rocks the third-sex lovers lined up against the street windows. Instead of looking out onto the fantastical tropics of Macao, they see a homeland of yellow cabs and Midwestern boys with swollen hormonal breasts. I rhyme with the chants until the music starts playing and Mario strolls over to kiss my ear, aiming intuitively through burnt red eyes. In '59 we'd been kids together on John R and Brush in Detroit, playing *bobo-bedetton-dotton* games with sticks, balls and jump ropes. Half the snowfiends in the club are from blocks like mine, and although some might say I fucked destiny standing up, I could still catch the disease. The sandy-haired girl with the translucent skin was probably destined for the Henderson, North Carolina Junior League and she's caught it. Mario calls her Pandy.

I look more closely at this girl Pandy. She wants me to watch her, and for a moment it's as if I'm in the presence of royalty, the red and blue lights of Said's reaching through her rich blonde curls and across the tiny features placed perfectly upon her Anglo-Saxon face. However, there is a trapped expression in Pandy's eyes as they embrace mine. She stands up and immediately I see that she is pregnant. Probably close to seven months. She is surrounded by the sycophants and true admirers of her court. The French silk and sequin shirt she wears covers her filled belly. She gracefully strides over to the dance floor. Her transition from empress to royal mother is effortless. It could humble the barren. She has engaged me without having to say a word. Mario says she always wears sequins. That she is referred to as the Sequin.

My eyes follow the Sequin's stride to the middle of the neon room where she automatically demands center spot. Her competition plays fierce and violent around her for a few minutes until it is absorbed into her dance. Joyfully the other dancers join the girl, not puzzled in the slightest by her grace and agility. She has two partners, likewise her partners, seven in all trading off girl for boy, boy for girl—little ambidextrous babies riding high on the mania of pills and madness. They dance fast. Jerky to the beat, step to step on sparkling shoes with stilt-heels, dervish turns Latin style, calling out high-pitched expletives meant to dot the same place in each skull. I watch the naked backs of the dancing boys, their greased spines like healthy roots, my eyes clinging tenuously to their ancient strength. Go down, go down on your boy, hump him from the back, hump him in the front—girl to girl, belly to belly, boy to boy up to down—fast now—not Latin erotic-smooth—fast bumping here and there, fast computer motions clicking on the upstroke, a slighter downbeat, bent knees, flamboyant male arms, rigid but cool female arms.

Pandy's earthbound body compels her partners to remain fixed. The floor chants, *She's so cool, she's icebox cool*. Little thirteen-year-old girls undulate involuntarily on the sidelines, their firm young bodies seasonally in need of the bizarre, calling back *I'm so cool, I'm icebox cool*, while their boys move next to them—each forsaking the other with the fantasy of making it with this sequined mothergirl and her androgynous entourage. I smirk at her glitter but its blood-color takes me captive. I fight her glory, yet her urgency wins. It might be the coke, or it might be that we each know about stepping out of one world into others, being watched as travelers always in between, claiming a love or a hate for some recent home whose legacy we daily tangle into more lie than truth. Or it might be that our lives intersect at a place beyond the gypsies, who, afoot for the spring thaw, remind us both that rebirth applies to all things. Whatever it is, she's taken my night from me, and maybe more.

A little girl painted head-to-toe in white paint over her dark skin, wearing a black hood over her hair, pasties over her breasts and a g-string-like facade over her tiny cunt, grabs my hand suddenly and pulls me out to the dance floor. She doesn't belong here. Someone must have brought her as a mascot, a cruel joke. She belongs downtown. Mario grins as she high-steps smoothly around me, softly leading me into a sensual counterpoint to the erratic moves of the dancers around us. We dance a slow hypnotic grind at first, half-time to the chant. Only our knees move, deliberately and in unison. The Sequin struts out and stands opposite us. Her stomach is thrust forward and proud. The seven-headed Dancing Machine stops to watch their girl come on cold. She is the star here. The Sequin turns her misshapen body to me, grasps me around the waist, and pulls me against her groin. I initiate a gesture of contempt, but knowing he has to get Pandy away from me fast, Mario slithers up laughing. He grabs Pandy around her waist and flips her toward him, twirling her the way a father would his child, gleefully offering a moment's different reality in the sweeping motion of a top, then releases her on the sideline before returning to me. Mario's attention has short-circuited the tension and the Sequin becomes no more than one of the sweet dancing girls I grew up with. The touch of a man has lessened the weight of her child so that she laughs as if through liquid. I continue to dance, waiting patiently while Mario slides down off his sloppy high. He holds me close as the song comes to its end.

Mario had been my first and I float along with that memory. He is tall and light-skinned. Almost pretty. Considered one of the lucky ones in those days. But he didn't deal in lucky. He had a brutal and facile mind. He chose me. I had style, no great beauty, but I could go toe-to-toe with him on any scheme. None of us thought he'd ever get hooked.

We dance until his eyes return to the bright they used to be after he'd beat me at stickball, and at the very moment this nostalgic mist could have turned into regret and accusation, Pandy touches me on the shoulder. Dugie takes you up and dugie takes you down, and part of the glitter of a sequin is the artificiality of its evanescence. I choose to sleep the tragedy of what has made me one thing and Mario a junkie, and decide instead to caress those blazing eyes that seem to leap from the dark rims set into Pandy's face. Drug solitude is common here, so I let her hold me from behind and dance with us.

I smell the rot of Pandy's imminent death. Someone else might miss the agony of her exile and sensationalize the choices she must have made, but I imagine that within Pandy's doom there is something pure and hyperbolic. There are separate, individual pains that are more vile in their means to exile than exile itself. It is an organic condition, not metaphor, and I want to flee from it. I want to walk right out of Said's and out of New York, out of the universe for that matter.

But instead, I take Pandy home with me that night, passing through streets littered with pigeon bone and bottle caps. My place is between Ninth and Tenth Avenues in the Fifties. As soon as we arrive Pandy uses my egg poacher as a cooker and shoots up at the kitchen table while we talk about setting the styles with rags, bandannas and secondhand acetate that Gucci later redesigns for the weary rich. As Pandy speaks, she plucks the air with her long fingers, drawing bows and barrettes and ankle bracelets on the air. I soon tire of her meanderings.

"Why are you having this baby? You're doing everything you possibly can to harm it."

She looks straight at me, not at all surprised by my brash change of subject.

"I'm not really a junkie. I just like to get high sometimes."

"All the time looks like to me."

"No, that's not really true. I go a day or two without nothin."

"Why do you say *nothin?* Was that the way you were taught to talk?"

"Don't be so hard on me. I'd like to be your friend."

"Sorry, I don't make friends easily. And they never make me."

I turn on her. She can't hold her head up any longer. She nods onto the table so I carry her to the chair and try to make her as comfortable as possible, surrounding her with old clothes I shape into pillows. I put a blanket my mother had left in the project when she died over Pandy's birdlike ankles and legs—they could have been my mother's. Pandy half dozes as I rinse out the dishes in the sink and prepare for bed. I'm angry with myself for finding her so compelling.

She startles me when she speaks out.

"Why did you cover my legs with the blanket and tuck me into a bed you made if you hate me?"

"I don't hate you, I just don't know what you want from me, and I know it's something."

The twilight color of predawn lights up one square foot of the rug in my first-floor room. Pandy leaves the nest I made her, twists her hair up into a little knot on top of her head and angles around the room. I light a joint and sit on the edge of my bed, following her transit across the floor. She watches me a minute. I don't say anything. Finally she does.

"You know, I used to be a cheerleader."

"So did I."

I can visualize Pandy's light hair in a flip and her lithe body wrapped in a red uniform as a highlight to the Henderson, North Carolina School Yearbook.

I am hooked by her vulnerability and decay in the same way I was by my mother's in the days before her death. But their decay is also my anger and defense. My mother's swollen alcoholic belly pressing against an organ that eventually turned her yellow and filled her tissues with the excrement of a body gone mad was my ticket out.

I decide to get ready for bed. I go first into the little room that holds the toilet, strip and grab a towel from the closet, then out to the screened-in area around the sink and bathtub. I stay behind the matchstick curtains for an unusually long time. Still, Pandy is not asleep when I pull the blanket back on my bed.

She whispers into the stale air, "I'll take you home with me tomorrow night."

Her unpredictability is as engaging as her vulnerability. Again, reminiscent. I would pay a lot of money if this were not the case. If I could resist.

In the morning I leave at my usual time, tired, but this isn't the first time. I trust Pandy to be there with nothing missing when I return in the evening. Our intimacy is automatic and, for me, uncomfortable. That night when I come home, she is dressed up in a plaid pleated skirt designed in such a way that she barely looks pregnant. She is a very small woman anyway. Her baby looks like it might be as well. She has cleaned my apartment, probably shot up for the day, been to her own place and gone shopping.

"You're coming over for dinner."

I'm not wild about the idea but decide to go anyway. We take the IRT express up to '25th and then walk crosstown. I don't know East Harlem all that well and the further east we go, the more uneasy I become. We don't talk much. We zigzag uptown, turn off the avenue and onto an unpaved, muddy street, heading toward the East River. We could be anywhere. Empty lots filled with city weeds and brick dust shroud the uneven boundaries of the street. I notice the wild dogs snarling in harmony when we pass them in the brush.

We leave the path, abandoned totally now by the city's compass of light. Pandy strikes a match and pokes her foot into the familiar earth as we continue to walk. Eventually we hit metal. I assume it is the old tracks from trains that used to carry the rich out of the city. Along the tracks a cement slab interrupted by periodic holes covered with gratings gives Pandy the direction she needs. The only peculiarity that makes these openings different from sewer covers is the large padlocks evidently holding sections of the gratings together. Pandy takes out a cylindrical key and opens one of these locks. She does it with a brief finesse that claims it as her home.

Pandy lifts the city grate up and drops it against the cement, then unlocks another padlock and shoves something heavy and metal inward. A gaslight globe lights our way down a flight of cement steps which opens onto a cave charmed only slightly by the touch of humanity. I notice the lamp immediately. The floor is packed mud, the walls cinder block, and in the center a small generator Pandy has switched on offers a glitter to the room. There is no bathroom. The generator seems also to hype up an hydraulic pump that brings water to a tiny sink Pandy uses to wash her hands and to pee in. The lamp possesses one corner, a bentwood rocker belonging in a young married's apartment another, a pile of neatly folded clothing the third; and finally, standing on an orange crate is a bowl filled with goldfish floating in scummy water. Her winter pets. The bed is swung up against the wall exposing bits and pieces of fabric draped onto the wire tapestry at odd intervals. Between the aquarium and the clothes, a metal door covered with posters of dark, dead jazz musicians stands ajar.

"Come and see the neighborhood."

"Is this where you live all the time?"

"It's my home, if that's what you mean."

The doorway leads out to the old subway tracks unused by the city since the twenties. The backs of an entire community of these part-mud, part-cement huts, all with doorways leading out to the tracks, line the ledge that eventually falls off into the pit of dead rails. From the stench it is obvious that this area is used for all forms of refuse, consumed daily by the rats that now slink around our legs.

I know rats. I move cautiously, remembering their feel on my face babied with milk, back in Detroit. Here the constant motion their squat bodies create imprisons me. In fact, the tracks themselves are fur-lined with the backs of these Norwegian city squirrels used to eating babies' faces and the mothers' arms that hold them. The numbing calm of shock allows me a moment to adjust, yet even as I stand paralyzed, I can see that the rats are like pets in this neighborhood. Doglike in their sensibility, the rats know if they don't graze on the flesh of their strange life-fellows, they will be fed a daily menu of garbage and human feces. Whirring armies of flying beetles the size of small mice stop just short of attacking my head. I sense in their kingdom the same peculiar fear and curiosity the families of a small village might experience when confronted by a stranger. Although the insects don't bite, Pandy runs into her home and brings out a foul-smelling root that she smears over my head and hair. With the odor signaling my rite of passage into their ranks, they move away to sit happily on the backs of the rats dozing on the forgotten tracks. In this symbiotic hell of the cryptozoa, the bugs live off the maggots that spontaneously appear in the garbage the rats leave behind, and although my fascination impoverishes my fear, there exists a dread far beneath the surface that has to do with Pandy and her comfort at my being here with her.

Halfway down the tracks I can see a bonfire being fed rags by a man with thick dreadlocks. Pandy tentatively explains that the groups of people I now begin to see around other bonfires strung along the edge of the pit as it curves to the left would be outlawed up on the streets. The people in the nicer homes living within the cinder and mud igloos provide these people with food and necessities, even though the longer the outlaws remain, the less they desire anything but their own sludge fires, their own conversation and a meal every so often.

For several moments there is silence between Pandy and me. Pandy moves from foot to foot restlessly. It is a graceful gesture. Her limbs sway to a silent chorus. Then,

"You shocked by where I live?"

"Is that what you want me to be? Is that why you live here?"

Her glow fades as I continue.

"Look, I know you don't have to live like this—that dress you wore last night cost more than a year's rent on my apartment. You have antiques in your mud hut. What kind of joke are you playing on yourself and the people who have to live here?"

Pandy spreads her hands out in all directions.

"Why shouldn't I live like this if they do?"

I am not amused by martyrs—their innocence a luxury I could never afford.

"Come on, we're going to have a talk. All you are is a kid."

Narcotized though she is, she stands her ground. "But why? Why shouldn't I live like they do?" She won't budge.

I lose patience and shout, "What about that baby in your belly?"

I grab her by the hand, expecting resistance, and find that she has gone limp. Her acquiescence to me seems total, so I lead her back to her hut. The usual distance and tension the drugs maintain are gone, and within seconds it is as if she has entered a fugue state interrupted only slightly by confusion, not wanting to submit or admit to anything, but reticently allowing me to move her about.

When she starts to cry uncontrollably as I pack a few things in her hut, I can't understand the words she is trying to form. This abrupt shift in mood is all too sudden for me, yet I suspect she has been moving toward this crescendo since before we met. Meeting me was mere serendipity. Now it all fits.

I lock the door to her home and we take a subway back to my house. I hold her in the back of one of the cars. When I finally get to my apartment I stick her in the bathtub. Her full stomach looks hard and mottled, as if her own flesh is all that can protect the jewel lying hidden inside. I consider shooting her up with an I.V. of valium and demerol from the hospital, but the bath seems to be calming her down. She calls to me that she has to return to get her lamp, she never travels without it; and then she dopes herself. Finally I get her into my bed to rest.

She must have left after I went to buy food at the Ninth Avenue markets. When I come back and can't find her, I call Mario. If I have to return to her hut, I don't want to go alone. I tell him to meet me at 125th and First, we can walk from there.

Mario is drugged to a fine tuning and in complete control.

I don't have a landmark or a key so when I find the gratings, I start knocking. The silence beyond each padlock does not unnerve me. I walk five blocks and, like a machine programmed for solution, I keep knocking and screaming Pandy's name. Mario follows me. We cross a patch that looks familiar. There is a stark sapling standing cold, new, out of place and memorable for its solitude—and the bricks some caretaker has built around it—in the middle of the path. I wait. I think I hear the tinny sound of a transistor radio.

Mario sucks the wind through his teeth as I holler, the matches burning in my fist illuminating the ground around us and one of the padlocked grates. All at once the noise stops and the grate is thrown open so suddenly that the only thing I glimpse is a dark head as it descends some steps into a pit below. Words pierce the darkness.

"All right. All right. My baby is me."

I follow the hysterical cries down the steps, turning around three times to beckon Mario to follow. He stands riveted to the clammy slab of cement, as if he is a watchdog bred in the bushes with the other wild dogs. He tells me to wait for him, but instead I continue into the deep black room at the bottom of the steps. I light another match and glance quickly around to get my bearings. The room is empty except for a sink like the one at Pandy's and a cot shoved up against the wall. The person who opened the door squats in the middle of the floor, cuddling what I presume to be an infant and screeching a lullaby in that high-pitched voice I mistook for a small radio.

The blanket swaddling the infant looks familiar. It takes a few minutes for my eyes to adjust to the lack of light, but gradually I can discern color and detail. An orange glow shines under the bottom and through the sides of the back door, stippling the mud floor around the woman. Pandy's neighbor holds a light brown child mottled from new birth. I feel very afraid. The neighbor is an old black-skinned woman with a goiter that hangs down to her breast where she is trying to suckle the child. The taunting shriek announces her insanity less vividly than the look in her eyes. "It's my baby see, it's my baby, please, you can't have my baby, my baby is me."

The old woman repeats the singsong over and over again. She pulls at the extra skin hanging from beneath her chin as the rhyme becomes a hymnal refrain. I step back and glance up to see if Mario is still at the top of the stairs, but he has already be-gun his slow descent. Obviously the sounds from below have both alerted and disoriented him. Like a night animal, once his eyes can make use of the available light, he adjusts to the situation. He sees my fear. In a guttural voice pitched against the noise of the old woman, he speaks to me.

"Get the fuck outta here. I'll help her. Get the fuck outta here!"

"Ask her about Pandy, please ask her."

I hear Mario from the twilight.

"If you don't get outta here, I'll walk right out and leave you *and* Pandy."

Mario stalks the distance between this creature and myself with an exorbitant hatred toward me for getting him into the mess. Out of habit, he begins rolling up his sleeves. When he is certain that the poor woman is reasonably harmless, although unpredictable, he very calmly addresses her.

"*Por favor, dónde está su amiga Pandy?*"

I hadn't heard the Latin accent in her song. Mario stares kindly and repeats his sentence. I try to focus.

"*Por favor, dónde está su amiga Pandy?*"

Without missing a beat or altering her expression, the old woman drops the baby and jumps back, hissing the words of the hymn in Spanish. I run to the baby and discover it is very recently stillborn. The goiter flaps as the old woman takes off around the room. When she races to her sink in the corner, sticking first one leg and then the other into the bowl, I run out the back door which leads to the tracks. Mario follows. Without thinking, I run deep into the city behind the huts and don't stop until I feel safe. Mario grabs me. My fever makes me a dangerous friend. It matches the heat of the sludge-fires warming the dreadlocked men.

"Cut it out. What's happening to you? We're on a mission. Don't go *saditty* on me now."

Mario has reached far back into our past to criticize my fear of this place. I stare at him. In the glow of a hundred different bonfires I fight the demon that drives me to embrace a stranger's pain. Mario doesn't respond to my stillness. He is watching something over my shoulder. I twist around so fast I am thrown off balance and fall. The palms of my hands touch a thin layer of mud before sinking with the weight of my body into the hideous rat food. The immediate impact of the odor makes me cry out, just as a voice above me begins to speak. Squatting there, arms thrown back for support, vulnerable to the dungeon and its recent history, I begin to weep.

The voice offers me a rag. I feel a need to be proper.

"Oh, thank you."

I stand up and peer into the face of a man who could have been the shadow with the thick dreadlocks I saw yesterday down near the main bonfire. He nods to me and watches peacefully as I primly clean off my hands. He repeats the words he has spoken before, and this time I hear what he means.

"She left you a note."

"What do you mean—left?"

"She's dead. Do you want me to take you to her?"

"How do you know who I am?"

"She said you would be coming. She expected you."

"What about the old woman? She's got Pandy's baby."

"We'll take care of that here."

We follow the man through the tunnel, past clots of people, their yellow fire lighting our way and the activity of the nether world, past the old woman's screams, down to Pandy's house which I can now see is in a cul-de-sac where the direction of the old train track takes a sharp turn to the right. All of the houses on the same line with Pandy's have colorful flowerpots filled with plastic flowers outside their doors. Mario follows the rats with his eyes. He never stops and never asks a question. The bugs are clustered in halos over Mario's head and my own. Mario does not try to brush them away. He keeps his fists clenched and his arms free to swing. Pandy's back door is open. Inside, the single Murphy bed is suspended halfway to the floor, swinging gently to the rock of the subway rumble. The material covering the springs and legs is eaten away by rats. Earlier in the day Pandy told me that wherever she goes to stay she carries with her the bronze lamp given her by her grandmother. Here the piece is more a touch of art in a room made barren by deliberate poverty. The base is broad—and carved out in bronze, against the light shining through a red Tiffany glass, is a small lady carrying a parasol as she descends a flight of steps into a Japanese garden. It is the little red light that now illuminates Pandy hanging in the center of the room. A gnarl of veins bulges through her needle-pocked skin like a blue worm reappearing in the nape of her neck, in her arms and in her legs. Even the femoral artery in her groin is swollen.

Mario's nose begins to run as we three stand. Pandy's commotion is mostly over. The roar of a subway crossing town to head up to the Bronx echoes in another part of the catacombs. The immediate stillness is interrupted each time Mario sniffs. I shake a little, never taking my eyes from Pandy and the homely afterbirth which hangs from her.

The man is the first to speak, and he speaks to Mario.

"If you want to leave, I'll watch over your friend."

"No, there's no more either of us can do. I think we should both leave."

I know I have many things to do yet. "You leave. Don't worry. I'm not frightened."

"I can't just leave you."

"Please. I'd rather. And besides," I gesture to our guide, "he'll make sure nothing happens."

Mario nods to the man, walks up the cement steps with the keys to the padlocks the man has handed him, unclasps the lock to the metal door, then the one for the grating covering the door. He throws the keys back down to me at the bottom of the steps and climbs out, leaving the door open but closing the top grate. The man walks out the back door and stations himself next to it. I close that door and look again at Pandy. I stand on the orange crate that has held the dead goldfish and lift Pandy out of her noose. I pull the bed down and lay her on it. Her pink sheets are covered with little rosebuds.

Then, finally, I look at the note underneath the lamp. She bequeathed me her grandmother's lamp. She had believed we had a preordained connection so strong that the force of her death would make itself known to me through a means beyond logic and information. What kind of ritual execution had been in her mind I can only crudely imagine; however, she probably had made peace in her final bargain: if the baby survived, it was meant to and she had protected and nurtured it as far as she could; if the baby died, then it was meant to because her poison had already begun to enter it. Understanding this primitive gesture binds me to Pandy in a way she would have wanted. Yet seeing that she could go no further into motherhood than expectancy does not surprise me. The Dancing Machine could come to life for a night in the afterglow of medicine, but it could not share a life with her. She wouldn't have wanted it to become her language. She was alone. And she had chosen it that way.

Touched briefly by clarity earlier today, she had seemed to understand what her choices meant. While Pandy was taking her bath in my apartment, after she calmed down a bit, she began talking about things she had read back in the days when she kept books. I tried to encourage her to confide in me but before I could stop her she shot up right in the bathtub and what might have become an explanation turned into babble. Instead of speech she spoke in tongues made feathery by the legs of spiders she claimed to feel spilling and prancing through her veins. It was frustration that precipitated my leaving for the market. Yet now as I stand next to her nearly alive body, I remember from the rubble of her monologue that there was an intaglio engraved upon her life, and that it is in a similar design to mine.

I ask the subway man to take me down to the old woman's home. He explains to her for me that she will have to give the baby back. That we have come for the baby. A group of people gathers outside her door merely to overhear our conversation. They lean into each other for comfort in the way old ladies might hold hands on the street. The woman hides in a corner and begins to sing the hymn again as she performs the ritual of wrapping the dead infant in the blanket, rolling the baby this way and that, murmuring her refrain until all of the blanket is tucked and folded around the infant. It is a boy.

His little body stiffened into permanent innocence. I take him down to his mother's bed and fit him neatly inside the curve of her elbow.

I nod to the subway man and close the door to the rats. I put the groceries over my arm that Pandy bought earlier, pick up the lamp and climb the stairs. There is a picture of Stevie Wonder I hadn't noticed before, on the wall leading to the street. The photo is a familiar one—from the days when Yolanda beaded and wove his hair. Mario is waiting near the little sapling down the mud from me. I slam the street door onto the darkness inside and we decide to walk home. On Broadway a little gypsy girl comes up to us and offers Mario a plastic rose. I cook dinner with Pandy's groceries and Mario stays with me until I tell him to go. I put the lamp in the closet where my mother's blanket had been, and that is the end of it.

Mario is in the hospital today. Watershedding. He decided two days ago. He hadn't shot up for thirty-six hours and the pain was ripping his gut to hell. I went with him to the hospital and I'll see him again tonight. He'll be in a cell, screaming maybe, or perhaps silent. Then he'll get out. He's my homeboy.

MADONNA

S HE'D BEEN WRAPPED IN BLUE VELVET, Mr. Carver's little sister, Yvonne, when they found her. She was a secretary down on Centre Street, got the job after the New Deal let the floodgates down for soft-colored Negresses and a few others.

She was always gonna make it out she used to say. *Outta what*, her brother would say, and she'd say *this stinkin lousy evil waitin, lyin in the cut waitin, waitin for nothin, cept to be called bitch this and bitch that and bitch get your silly black ass back here—but I ain silly.*

No, Yvonne wasn't silly. But she was mad and there was no room for mad in the Carver family or any family from 52nd & 9th, Blues Street.

So she moved and when she moved she moved where there were white girls who laughed and hissed at her on the street, and where there wasn't a corner store. It didn't have the people she was used to, nobody like on Blues Street to praise her silken skin.

Got so nobody spoke to her. Got so men taunted her and women said they wanted her out of the neighborhood. Got so the white women were complaining to their men Queens was getting to be a little Africa.

The final cut went something like this.

The chocolate cream curve of her thigh could be seen just beneath the hem of the blue velvet, and, in the commotion of discovering her, when her bruised breast blossomed out from under the left lapel of the damp sleeping coat as if the milk of a century's women were pumping inside, the Italian cop who still lived with his parents up on 116th & 2nd moved toward her and covered the soft skin.

The blue of her velvet was the blue in the cape of a painting of the pregnant Madonna he had seen inside a chapel on an Italian hillside above a wine field. The Italian cop had been there just once. His grandmother had taken him in through the little side door and made him kneel on the freezing damp concrete. She put large coins into the little box and a light burst forth. On the stone wall the Madonna waited, stopped in time as if by miracle.

The Madonna had her finger just inside the front fold of her blue velvet as if unconsciously fingering the shape of the fetus floating suspended inside her womb. And he'd found her provocative, tantalizing, almost sexual in her coyness. Even a young boy could see that she knew who slept inside.

He thought he'd never see anything like her again. But then he got called on the 10-54 and walked inside this apartment smelling like the inside of three-week-old carrion with blood and shit splattered around like Hell had become a man and walked in the front door mad.

And there she was. The woman lying below him could have been the child born of that Madonna, each of their features so subtly Mediterranean, their eyes shaped like olives and their noses, as if plucked from the face of an Abyssinian princess, reaching down to the perfectly shaped dark rose lips.

One hand was twisted in bas-relief against the white and pink flowered sheets, that last instant claimed forever by the movement of her skinny arms. Urine simmered hot around her. It had been days, but the heat outside matched the heat of her body the second she died.

It was like being stretched out over a canvas that couldn't hold your image no matter what, she had been so afraid. That's just how afraid she must have been, the cop thought, like being stretched out over a canvas that couldn't hold your image, no matter what.

The other cops with him, his Irish partner and two others, played with her toes, used their heavy tie boots to play with her pussy. They had opened the blue velvet. He couldn't stand it. They flashed back the part of the lapel he had flapped closed when he first had seen her, and they fondled her breast.

The little guinea cop went crazy then. That's how Mr. Carver, Yvonne's brother, tells it. *He started shooting bullets through the ceiling and started screaming nigger-lover cop cunt Mother Mary full of grace* over and over until the other cops got worried and went about their business reporting on a suicide, ignoring the bruises and the blood and Hell at Booth and Main, Flushing Meadows, Queens.

The stench had hit the streets and when the screams came the white girls who lived in the houses around the neighborhood had to say what they had to say—

The young police officer never went back to the 110th precinct. He went looking for Yvonne's family and when he found Mr. Carver he stayed with him.

He said *maybe that man who painted pregnant Mother Marys full of grace on cold walls knew what it was to wrap a nigger bitch around your waist and squeeze her mother breasts and buttocks until the cream of those centuries burst forth and she cried until she couldn't cry anymore, just like your sister cried.*

Mr. Carver says it was all he could do *to keep from killing the little guinea when he called his sister a nigger and talked sex about her.* But Mr. Carver was a thinking man and throughout the first telling of the whole story, when the Italian cop told Mr. Carver, Mr. Carver kept thinking and waiting.

He let the cop talk. He wanted to hear it all. But more than that, something touched there, just for a moment, yet for a long enough moment to let the cop tell the story, because otherwise Mr. Carver would've had to kill the cop.

But something told him that this cop would have a hard time trying to forget his little sister's twisted help-me-please body. And now it is that Mr. Carver has the whole story to tell, not the reported version. And now it is too that when Mr. Carver tells the story, he also says how *it all comes down to the personal, as huge as the thing really is. Especially at the kill.*

RED GABLES

A MUTED KNOCKING SOUND DRAWS HER
to the left side of the pond, calling her to a
place of slow motion and pounding. Hugh's
*fists thump the quilt of frozen water keeping him from
Cristina, while his eyes search the underside of the
ice she is held up by. His throat cannot form a noise
shrill enough to pierce the element gone wild with
natural change.*

*Cristina steps onto the ice above her father's fig-
ure. His powerlessness leaves her mind with the short-
ened gasps of vision that replace all thought before
death. She sees him thrust his hands, palms up,
against the ice and motion for her to point in a direction that will enable him to return to the element
that understands the way he works. It eases her to
believe that even now he has the situation under*

control. *Eager for the task, using her fingers as a diviner's rod, she traces a line in the ice to a spot on the pond where the ice is punctured and cracked.*

The familiar pond decorates the center of the kitchen window where minutes ago Cristina had been standing, preparing the noon meal. As she trussed the young hen she and her father would eat in another hour, she glanced outside, her mind instinctively seeking his dark face. When it happened, it seemed as if a magnet drew him deep into the icy black water. He had been checking the ice for weak spots where he could carve a fishing hole. It was the warmest winter on record in the small almost Southern town, which meant the fish—as Cristina imagined it—might not have all gone downstream into the rivers and gulf.

He had easily cracked open the surface of the water before slipping. Two weeks before, when the twilight Hugh returned in was green with news of early spring tornados, the creek that fed the enormous fire pond outside the kitchen window rumbled outraged beneath what he had thought was a thin coating of ice. Nature had played another trick on him by making the ice floes thicker and more lively than they appeared. His head bobs, fighting something; and then he disappears, the ice mysteriously, almost purposefully closing over the hole, as if this one small act of trespass provoked an anger at his presence sufficient to eliminate him. But the anticipation that in another few hours they would be admiring her father's strength and laughing at the pond's silly attempt to kill him drove Cristina forward, her blue feet and exposed shoulders becoming like boils in the bitter wet wind. She was a child again, expecting to see her father rise like a mighty pharaoh from his premature sarcophagus.

Always Hugh had fought off terror with brute strength and deliberate misinterpretation, leading his daughter to believe he had been given a "foreknowledge" that allowed him to strong-arm the world and those he loved. Such portentous knowledge comforted her in the early years of her mother's illness. As a child she had been told that her mother slept so peacefully because she was waiting. Sometimes Cristina would stand in the doorway of the faded room of the upstairs sitting parlor and watch her mother—so soft and untouchable was her thin sympathetic face against the pillow shams on the canopy bed that Cristina, with grave certainty, eagerly anticipated the time when she would become a woman with a child and fall into the same slumber.

The servants whispered and touched one another if they passed Cristina in the hallway off her mother's rooms, not one of them ever daring to take Cristina aside and explain away the legend of the woman's slumber. Cristina's world had consisted solely of her mother, her father—Hugh—and the servants: servants who were self-explanatory, a father who fed his child and took her on small trips, and a mother who slept with god and would someday be wise enough to pass on to her the secret of birth. Later there would be her Nana.

When Cristina was a child, there had been an aviary behind the main house where the redbirds and the bluebirds and mourning doves, who preened themselves in the marbled baths covering the grounds, stayed the day grazing beneath the overflowing feeders. Hugh would take Cristina to the woods behind the dam and teach her how to shoot a bow and arrow. As she grew in age and understanding, her mother's illness was never mentioned. The only fact that surfaced was that her mother had not been well since giving birth.

Cristina would look into the face lying on the ironed fresh pillow sham and see that in some miraculous way, without the disadvantage of movement or exposure, the face grew older, yet more beautiful. Cristina wondered if it was Hugh who removed her night garments and positioned her face toward the sunny window each morning. There had always been some sort of nurse in the background, living in a small room off other small rooms. The blondness of her mother's hair sometimes turned dusty, but Cristina suspected her father colored it during the hours when the house was asleep, because the original luster would return on a regular basis.

Only once had Cristina noticed her father with her mother. She was approaching the sitting room to peek in on her mother very early one morning. She hadn't slept well the night before and finally had dreamed of her mother's silk nightgown, perfectly formed in the shape of a woman, drowning in a bath prepared for Cristina. When she woke she needed to see her mother immediately. She rushed down the hallway, but in nearing the door, she heard murmurings. They were her father's. She couldn't bear to hear what he thought, what he whispered to his wife in the solitude of their wedlock. She had fled back to her room.

The interior quality of the mother's existence left the father and daughter with nothing mundane to say. Hugh never made an attempt at superficial explanation once Cristina was old enough to comprehend the fallacy of the legend she had been recited as a child. On anything further, Hugh maintained a deep silence so striking Cristina never dared try to break it. Nevertheless she believed her mother understood her own life, its surroundings, the murmurings of her husband and later the conversations Cristina initiated.

It was when Cristina had just passed her twelfth birthday that she noticed the changes in her own body. They delighted her in the way a short but perfect waltz she composed on the piano had once delighted her. It had been a sparkling melody with a tumultuous undertow in triple measure time. She mistakenly played it for her tutor who promptly asked her to perform the piece at the next recital in town. The tutor no doubt had not meant to be intrusive, but naturally Cristina was horrified by such a provocative request, declined and silently took note not to permit anyone ever again to know of her private creations. She felt similarly about the changes she was unintentionally creating in her own body.

She wondered then about Hugh in a new way the changes made possible. The meaning of companionship was unclear to her; what it was that her confusion manifested must have become noticeable to Hugh, and abruptly Cristina's one friend withdrew. For months, both father and daughter lived under the tyranny of puzzlement. Cristina was not certain why, but a very deep and silent epiphany took place which made her shudder. Hugh said he must leave for the city on business and that Nana would be staying with Cristina for a while. Hugh did not return, but Nana helped Cristina grow.

Nana's features were delicate and the white hair thin—it had tumbled down into thick blonde waist-curls when she had been a girl herself. That first winter with Cristina, her shapely extended fingers had already started to knob at the joints, but she was every touch the lady she had been at thirty-two when she married: corset, chemise, camisoles, stockings, layer upon layer of undergarments made pink-clean and perfumey-ready the night before in preparation for each day. There were earrings and a brooch to match the dress of the day—she had never worn a pair of slacks in her life, even as a child—and she expected Cristina to dress for supper every evening.

One night Cristina, as a test more than a rebellion, wore blue jeans to the dinner table. Nana refused to serve. The two sat in silence. There was no rudeness between them. The spring sun had left a flaming orange plume across the bottom half of the sky and the shadows cast from the tall-backed Empire dining chairs facing the floor-length leaded glass window deepened with each minute. Nana never moved. She played with the sterling napkin ring—her nobly long fingers a distraction from the back of her hands, just slightly spotted with rust. She never once looked at Cristina. She gazed into the disappearing sun and clucked to the birds clutching the wrought-iron railing of the adjacent terrace. At the half hour, Cristina slipped out from her seat and walked silently past Nana to her room to change into a spring print dress and low heels. When she returned, they talked about which of Nana's birds would stay for the summer solstice.

In October of Cristina's seventeenth year, Hugh returned. He let himself in the front door. Nana and Cristina were eating in the dining room. His hair was thick black with white streaks at the temples. Without a word he walked over to what Nana called the Victrola. Cristina had rarely been in the presence of her father when there was no music: as he would tell her, even in the woods the music of the trees and wind and birdsong clustered about his ears. Afflictions Cristina never contemplated had brought her father to an understanding of the gruesome in life so that his eyes were the only lightness that unexpectedly cut an enchanted flash of joy across an otherwise cynical face. Cristina's mother had been as light as her father dark, and the combination gave Cristina an almost Mediterranean cast to her skin.

Cristina had never seen the limp. She jumped up. Then stopped short of running to him when she saw him wince. He looked to Nana for help. The two seemed to have an understanding of a depth that left Cristina feeling like an outsider. Red Gables had been given to Hugh by Nana's husband, who built it for his wife and baby daughter many, many years ago.

"Why didn't you tell us you were coming, Hugh?"

He subtly dipped his head. The gesture moved Cristina. This was her father. Back for her!

"I know I should have called to let you know."

"Will you be staying long?"

Forever, Cristina prayed.

"Probably not."

Nana gazed past him out the bay window to her birds. Cristina stared at Hugh. She was a grown woman now.

"Say hello to the child, Hugh," said Nana without diverting her gaze.

There was silence. No one would look at Cristina. She continued to stare at her father. The gray under his eyes enhanced the sensuality in his face. He looked like the Europeans she'd seen in the fashion magazines Nana permitted her to buy at Ralston's once a month. In Cristina's dreams she and her father, if they were ever to see each other again, would either fall into each other's embrace, whispering the other's Christian name, or they would stalk one another like wild jungle beasts until Cristina leapt into her father's face and scratched his eyes.

The lids of Hugh's eyes suddenly snapped up. The unnatural loathing Cristina had dreaded for five years faced her now. Why else would he have abandoned her and her comatose mother if he had not hated them? When Hugh caught Cristina's expression, immediate comprehension crossed his brow, but it was too late. Cristina had run from the room. He had seen the creases of pain that were so characteristic of his own face beginning already on his daughter's, as if they were lines of a map collected in expectation of this time together.

Later that night Nana told Cristina she would be leaving for a while. Cristina did not respond to her Nana. She fled to her mother's room and told her everything that was happening to her and that no one could stop it. No one could rescue her from what was about to happen. This man "Hugh" her mother had married meant to sell their beautiful home, with its birds and birdsong and the animals that appropriately did not understand her language. Their lives had been exactly the way Cristina wanted and now change would destroy the delicately balanced ecology she had worked so hard at. Her father meant to sell her too, and her mother who slept on in the fresh linens.

Cristina spent two weeks impoverished by a tragic sense that had no focus, playing the piano every night before she and her father sat down to eat in silence, surrounded by their three lives together again. Her tears spilled mechanically. The quotidian of their profane trinity had not broken, even though Hugh still intended to sell Red Gables with Nana's blessings and send his daughter off to something different. This had been his plan anyway, but now he had to wait for Nana.

In the beginning, Hugh did not look Cristina in the face. He stayed in the guest room where there was a picture on the wall of him and his wife. He looked younger even than Cristina did now. He had expected to leave the day following his arrival. He had not wanted Nana to leave. He only wanted arrangements to be made and then executed. Nana knew better. There were other things to be attended to yet.

The first two days Cristina hung around outside Hugh's room without venturing in. She did not return on the third day. He came out of the room only for supper. He had not yet been to his wife's rooms. He spent time remembering how he had watched his wife slide deeper into the slumber that persisted still. There was a time when he believed she would awaken, and he spent that time dreaming. But the whiskey he had considered medicinal in the first years became more than a soft lace over his spirit. The whiskey had combined with his pain in such a way that his madness made him seem omnipotent, and his daughter's dependence became absolute. He could harm her by his presence. He had known when to leave. The decision to return was more difficult.

On the fourth day Hugh went into his wife's rooms and spoke to her. They had let her hair turn to a genteel dust befitting her age and station in life. But her face was as he expected, the high cheek-bones going skeletal and the skin beneath giving way ever so slightly, year by year. He spoke that night to Cristina over his dinner.

"Your face was stolen from your mother's."

"Am I pretty then?"

Hugh did not say anything for a long time. He turned his face to Cristina's, but the darkness she had so easily become accustomed to protected his expression. He had a low, smooth voice—it contained a power.

"I can't answer that."

Days went by and father and daughter did not speak of departure or selling. In tacit agreement, they allowed their lives to be drawn in by the silent routine and dailiness of the house. Hugh spent hours speaking with his wife. Cristina feared they spoke of an imminent sale. She went to her mother in the late hours and pleaded with her to somehow dissuade this man from taking away their only refuge. Her mother's body would sometimes twist and rise up when Cristina spoke. What would they do if they left? Live as Hugh must have lived, in rooms off other rooms, like their servants? In cities she and her mother had not been to, sharing rooms with people they did not know? There could be no other home but Red Gables. Their future had to lie in the depths of the house, its trees and animals. Cristina urged her mother to see the logic of it.

Cristina let the staff go without telling her mother or her father, or calling Nana. She explained to the old-timers that they could consider it a temporary vacation. Together she and her father would have to be bound to keeping up Red Gables. Cristina began doing the things she had seen her servants do. She cooked the meals and cleaned the special things, like the graceful mahogany end table that had a treble clef sign as a brace. It held the twenty-four-karat bookends separated by a single volume of Bobby Burns.

For several more days, Hugh stayed inside his room, venturing out only to see his wife and to dine with his daughter. He hadn't spoken again. And Cristina had not returned to his room.

One very bleak night, Cristina switched on the hall light down from Hugh's room because she had seen a light from underneath his door. She turned the light on to see if he would turn his off in an effort to avoid her knowing he was still awake. He did not. So she flipped the switch back off and opened the door to his room.

He looked straight at her this time.

"You've come back. I know what you're doing."

"Yes."

"You're very young to be so capable."

"I had to learn early. That's okay."

"What's the date today?"

"It's March eighth."

"I felt you'd come back."

"Yes."

"Your birthday is a week from today. The Ides."

"Yes."

"Downstairs in the boxes I brought with me are the operas. We will start tomorrow night with *La Bohème* and see how many days it takes us to finish. Then we will decide what is to be."

Hugh began working on the frozen landscape, examining the pond for the pickerel darting through the muddy waters beneath the ice. He looked forward to waking into the brisk morning chill that took him out to the fire pond where he maintained an inexplicable vigilance while chopping at the ice. Meanwhile, Cristina searched everywhere for the recipes said to have been her mother's favorites before the illness. Pastas covered with sauces of olives and ricotta, gumbos with authentic *filé*, arugula salad and roasts spiced with garlic and rosemary were addressed with great precision in a special pantry file. Nana had never shown her these things. The local grocer thought arugula and *filé* might be roots nurtured in the south for voodoo ritual, so Cristina consulted a dictionary and discovered her mother must have traveled. Cristina spent hours in the basement, savoring the musty earth smell of the clay and stone structure upon which the house was built. There was a crawlspace behind the old coal-burning furnace where she would sit, planning the evening meals.

When Cristina wasn't cooking, she was restoring the house to the way she remembered it before Nana took over, assuming it was her mother who originally organized the home as it had been in Cristina's childhood. The rooms still held that special sweet aroma she associated with an earlier Red Gables; it was the scent that was companion to the mental minuet she had danced with her parents since long before her father's leaving.

Each night for six days, father and daughter sat and sometimes paced at the mother's bedside, listening to a different opera. They listened to *La Bohème*, *Tosca*, *La Forza del Destino*, *Aida*, *Pagliacci*. On the sixth night they took in *Turandot* as eavesdroppers to an earlier year when Hugh had taught Cristina its arias as a child. Cristina wept. They never spoke. The darkness grew to be a fourth presence.

On the first night as Bergonzi sang "Che gelida manina," Hugh had gripped Cristina's hand and held it. It was the only time he had touched her since she was a child. He caressed the side of her face and then his wife's face, and before the opera was over, he left the room. Cristina stayed with her mother that night, sleeping next to her warm body.

On the sixth day Hugh had skirted the pond as Cristina watched from the kitchen window. He had told Cristina over supper before going to her mother's rooms that even though she had never seen her mother marching around, or tilting her head back just so when finishing a task, thinking before she spoke—even though Cristina had never seen any of these things, she nevertheless had taken on the expression and posture of her mother. What he did not say was that he had watched the spirit of his bride smolder mutely inside his daughter who had never met her mother, and that the similarity lay in something not controlled by man or reason.

That night, Cristina stayed again with her mother, falling asleep thinking that the next night she would hear the "Liebestod" from *Tristan und Isolde*; they had saved her favorite opera for last. For her birthday. She felt her mother twisting in the night, as if in dream, and later her father's presence.

Cristina jumps on the ice. The more vigorously she motions and draws her father's eyes to the opening, the further he falls away from her. The ice seems to have become looking-glass and she the mirror image of herself. Her father moves in the wrong direction, his red plaid shirt shifting up to cover his face. She tries pointing in the direction opposite where he should be floating and he sinks diagonally away from her. She screams at him, pleading with him to understand her words, but his eyes are now watching her through a silver glaze that has already captured his senses and is taking him deeper into the pond where green lily pads will hatch for the summer and where fish eggs wait for the spring sun to give them birth. He sees a dark-haired girl with gypsy skin belly flop on the surface of the ice, staring at him importunately and with a propriety that has no meaning to him as he settles into the logic of dying.

Cristina felt her mother's presence enter her dreams and awakened abruptly as a remote tremor told her that the relationship between herself and the figure in the red Pendleton shirt disappearing beneath the ice of the fire pond existed only for her. She shook herself completely awake so that the power of her mother's thoughts would not draw her back into the dream until it became no longer a dream. Cristina stealthily left her mother's rooms and returned to her own.

As an afterthought she turned and walked back to the other wing of the house where her father's room was located. She entered the room and sat on the edge of the bed. She looked at where her father lay so still and in her memory she heard the

"Liebestod." In that instant she knew her father had come home to die. She understood many things better now. His leaving and his not coming back. Even things perhaps he hadn't understood. Like her mother's power; he might not have known about that. In fact, for all he might have known, he really had come home intending to sell.

Her heart pounded her breast, which she clutched to prevent something so riotous from disturbing the moment. She heard the "Love Death" as if it were in the next room, and then she heard the silence.

Cristina woke up in her blue and green fresh room. Nana was sitting on the edge of the canopy bed. They were covered by a garland of blue violets on white organdy lace.

"He's dead."

"Yes sweetheart. It's over."

"Where was he?"

"We found him next to you."

"How did he do it?"

"Don't be morbid. It's over. You must stop thinking about him and get on."

"With what?"

"Growing up."

"I loved him."

"So did your mother. It's over now."

SURVIVORS

S HE DIED ON VACATION. MY MOTHER DID.
I was ten. I was convinced her body was
swollen with sea monsters that had crept in
while she was floating on a crest of turquoise foam
and had weighted her down into the reefs off Negril
Beach. The turbulence that hit the country roads that
night left the same taste of brine on my lips as hers.
I rode in the back of the truck, deftly knotting her
hair to each finger of my one hand while the fingers
of the other locked into hers. The dampness was
soothing. It surrounded me and comforted me to think
I smelled what she must. When we reached the hospital in Montego Bay I stood outside, sprayed with a
salty mist that corroded my skin, waiting for the car
that would bring my grandmother down from her

glass house in the hills. There was a nightclub in the distance, across the sand from where I stood. Lights pulsed through its windows with an arrogance that competed with the gods I needed on that storm-filled, starless night. Its existence was erotic and compelling. I could almost hear the music. The stage was a cement slab shot with a bullet of light that pinned down the shape of a beautiful woman. But the woman broke from the light and, instead of being its slave, made the light track her across the stage. There was a darkness to her. She was bare-foot, white gauze circling her body, pieces stretching down near the ankle then swooping up to catch a bone-shaped shoulder the color of rose caramel. It was my mother. She pressed her hips out to the audience forcing the light to spread over the rage in her body. Then suddenly the tempo picked up quixotically, as if I were not controlling the rhythm after all, and parted me from my mother's solemn expression. And I heard the wheels of my grandmother's car tear up the parking lot.

Lounging in my apartment in New York now, I think back on the girl who could have been a care-free debutante in Chagrin Falls, waiting for the afternoon's swim party at the country club before the dinner-dance that night at Lynnie's pony farm. I look at my hands especially, the wrists too and then the ankles and front bones of my legs. Under translucent skin, the delicate bones in the front, hiding veins, seem so vulnerable still. They don't appear as mine. They belong to a *Vogue* cover girl of the forties. Tonight I wear pleated white shorts, a jersey cloth pullover made to look as casual as a T-shirt, and a drape of silk fabric padded in the shoulders, rounded "just so" down the arms and swooping to a finish just below the shorts. I am sitting on the Queen Anne wing chair with one leg draped over an arm, and I am waiting for a rush. In these moments I cannot conjure up the differences between what I've become and the debutante my grandmother wanted me to be. I am both, or I am either, until the warmth in my veins transforms to a power that takes over, and I am everybody and everything and more than that debutante could have ever hoped to be. And far less.

Earlier this evening when I leaned in slow motion to turn on my lamp, the evenness of the smoky late dusk light was thrown off balance by the stark shadows dusted by the naked lamp bulb. It's easier for me to get up late. I don't want to think about all the morning people meeting over cups of coffee, doing everyday things, even important things. For those first minutes of near waking, before my temperature rises and my body's gripped by the panic, there is a fleeting glimpse of who I once was. It's a feeling not unlike the first rush, strong and self-assured. My mother used to say the reason she woke up frantic was plain and simple. It's death. Awakening from death is monstrously electrifying. She was on cruise control with a sonic boom in her chest, just like me. But if she was saying that the transition from sleep to waking was too much to bear, all I can say is that it is the only thing I *can* bear. With the movement from one kind of reasoning to the next comes forgetting.

Listen. There's this sound. If Mama were Sound she'd be this sound. It's soft and reminds me of the excitement of hot weather, summer night. A girl swaying, hips one way, arms the other, to this sound, on a stoop up on St. Nicholas, say around 143rd. Her dance is that moment a painting catches of city children, on a beach like Rockaway, subway-close, at the finish of a day, moving knees and pelvis against each other, individual units of two with balanced shoulders high and subtle in their reach for the rhythm coming from the radio, Smokey or Curtis, maybe even Clyde in the old days, under the bright twilight of a summer sky. The boys have their T-shirts thrown over their right shoulders, one hand held in place and ready to rumble, the other wound around their girls. I feel their groins in mine, grinding through their tight cheap pants into my light summer sundress. I remember the heat on Soundview

Avenue and the unironed red blouse I'm wearing as I carry a baby across the street to the liquor store to find my mother. My mother's pretty light brown skin is flushed and spotted from too much gin and a life of leaning into defeat. I remember the baby as a sister, or other close relation.

But Mama's never been to Soundview Avenue in the Bronx or 143rd and St. Nicholas in Harlem, and I don't have a sister. I grew up on golf courses and in swimming pools whose air-conditioned clubhouses were built by the ancestors of my boyfriends. My forays out of my world are contrived. Not that Mama wouldn't have understood.

The memory of my mother's big fluff of strong black hair she rolled into all sorts of styles when she left the house—it was allowed to cast wildly about when we were home alone—strikes me every time I comb the wavy blonde hair I inherited from my father. My mother's dark fullness was a contrast to my slim fairness. I recall only a sense of her, and that a dramatic quality I associated with passion and despair still surrounded her when she died. The one memorable feature of my father's very early departure seemed to be the way my mother leapt into her life with me as if we were childhood friends rediscovering each other later in life. As if we needed to return automatically to our patterns of unspoken secrecy and urgent dependence—

intimacies that could not be shared before he left. Yet I say all this now, of course, with a distance that has taught me how to appreciate her drama and why its urgency compelled me. I was meant to carry on the historic legacy of my grandmother's family with features more compatible to the current surroundings by virtue of my father's blonde curls so common amongst the Ashkenazi of his heritage. My mother had been the picture of her mother when each was thirty-four, Mama's death age; yet my mother's life was a kind of tenancy to my ownership of the family future. She lived at angle to that which I was meant to embrace.

I remember it was the familiar perfume of snow pine that greeted my grandmother and me as the car glided past the electric gate and up the driveway to the house the day after Mama's funeral. Once inside the center hallway of the grand old family home, grandmother gracefully bent at the knees and began to roll up the rust and blood-orange kilim that spilled over the special inlaid border of the parquet floor. Grandmother had imported from France all of the pieces of antique wood and ivory making up the border, and had designed the inlay herself. When my mother became mistress of the house, she exiled to the attic the pearl and blue Persian runner that belonged neatly inside the intricate border, not just for reasons of perversion but also because the ornamental things of life, made symbolic by the ceremony or rite of passage for which each was created, had more to do with the way she lived her life than did my grandmother's sense of civilized beauty. My mother found the revelatory epiphany of the Baptist in many things. There were masks from the menstrual huts built for the women in the New Guinea highlands, a Shoshoni totem pole covered with the symbols of movement, ancient Semitic tribal capes, Cyrius stars the Sephardics wore before the Star of David, Coptic crosses and Muslim fighting spears used against the Ethiopian Christians, lions of the desert. Her *pièce de résistance* was the cassowary beak brilliantly painted by some Papuan Indians whose dyes stood out in startling contrast to the one watercolor by Monet Mama had left in the living room as being representative of her Western cultural roots. She traveled like a diasporic gypsy to discover her artifacts, leaving no aromatic odor or souk unexplored.

Of course her ways of being were partly affectation. But for now, I can't stand hearing the soft excitement of hot-weather-sound because it moves into a memory of her—because it is the sound I have decided to associate with her for reasons that seem primordial, unavailable, inescapable. She might have chosen Cajun for me—or reggae. Or maybe something wilder. I hear the Sound like I see her exotic dance. It would be different if I could just disappear into the Sound and some braided girl's dance, and be only the movement in the girl's hips, following the Sound through the bodies of all the girl's friends. I live in my *fantasia*, sometimes aided by a pill or two—or more—and to transform the recollections of the past into a fluid young street-girl dancing-move is better than remembering. Unfortunately for me, the function of memory that shields one from the quick-jab power of experience has not succeeded in making more poetic, more economical, the pain of that starless, briny night upon which my life is so deeply impaled.

There was one very special sitting room on the main floor of the house which Mama had never touched in her capricious restructuring of our home. When she would leave on the vacations she explained were only for "grown-ups," I would spend hours in this parlor, fondling the porcelains, held for their fragility inside a dark mahogany table, octagonal in shape, and whose deep sides and glass top are framed in ivory. It stands next to my bed now. Located just underneath one corner of the ivory is a clasp I would unhook to open the top; and there, set like precious stones into a bed of moss-green velvet, lay treasure boxes of porcelain, each trimmed with a pink gold or a white gold or a sterling silver or a foreign metal I couldn't fathom. I would make up stories to go with each box.

My favorite story was of me going into a city to watch bare-breasted women lean from their broken wood-framed windows, calling for the night. As a child I'd read about places like that in Panama City and New Orleans and Istanbul. And I would imagine waiting in the slim alleys between their houses in anticipation of the dinner hour. At six-thirty the kitchen at the back of each house would fill with the women of the windows, great red and flabby women, skinny, pale and jumpy women, all dressed in white garters or white chemises or white lace panties, as they danced around, making a dinner of gumbo and dirty rice. They would fondle each other and joke about their indoor world, inside the houses with the windows on a street covered with sand and wild rose. There would be one girl, a very young girl, whom they would sometimes carry to the parlor and place on a chaise lounge and massage, as if she were special in that house. And finally at the end of their meal I would peek in the back window, dodging the white bloomers hanging from the clothesline, and whisper to this youngest girl, and she would turn and stare at me with her charcoal resonant eyes, so resonant it was as if nature had made a special category for them, and she would say, you wanna see magic, this is magic. Her voice was my mother's and it would tell me to go to the beach tent where the undenberry blossoms smelled of camomile and the fiery pakeef birds whispered thoughtlessly. And there on the beach, surrounded by water beasts, I would find the most beautiful dark wood box. Having never heard of an undenberry tree or a pakeef, I would watch myself run to the beach and search for the box I never found.

A silent fear kept me from opening any one of my family's boxes, so that I didn't discover for the longest time that inside each was a stone taken from the marriage rings of all the women in the family dating back to Renaissance Italy.

After Grandmother had rolled back Mama's kilim that day we returned from the funeral, she walked out into the winter light in the back orchard. I stood at the window and thought how the familiar span of wrought-iron fencing, gazebos, aquamarine pool colors and blue spruce, all peeping through miles of snow, probably implanted my first sense of winter light. Grandmother moved the bird feeder meant to tempt the robins and bluebirds nearer the gazebo where she would have the gardener lay traps for the grackles. When I descended the staircase for dinner later that evening, I saw that Grandmother had centered the cherry empire drop-leaf in the solarium off the dining area so that we might eat our first course to the timing of sunset. I recall the birds closing in on the warm smells and the familiar clicking of Grandmother's low heels which reminded me of the silent commotion I always sense just before the evening meal. The winter light settled in around me then and assured me of my permanence there. I was discomfited. Grandmother removed the chesterfield jacket to her purple suit and rolled the silk sleeves of her blouse above the elbow. In her exquisite way, she ladled out the rich soup and later served the delicate meat of the roasting hen. The servants had not yet returned.

For dessert she had selected one of the little boxes from the mahogany table. It was an especially pretty box with the tiniest rosebuds I had ever seen. She handed it to me. Each bud had been painted on as if by ancient Persian miniaturists and the box itself felt more crystal than porcelain. Grandmother had the same texture to her hair as my mother—its wildness tamed with combs and fastened into a bun—and the same patrician face, although its wisdom was rigid. There was the faintest touch of rust on one hand. She turned the box over in her hands and underneath, printed out in gold lettering, was Mama's name. I explained to Grandmother that my mother would have preferred a box brought up from the sea, where abalone and bottom feeders lived. We sat in silence then until the flaming orange

plume left by the sun was no more than a faraway
burning cinder.

I'm getting dressed now and I feel good. I'll end
up at Mikell's later so I've selected a pink silk chemise that, drifting over the jungle made by my blue,
orange and pink-purple Hermés pantyhose, is striking. The jewelry is all vintage Mama. The pills work
quickly on an empty stomach. At the kitchen sink I
wash two down with some cranberry juice, a multi-
vitamin and some bran while I watch the joggers
through my window as they cruise down the East
River boardwalk to Carl Schurz Park.

Outside on the corner of 79th and First I buy the
paper before going to Mikell's. I've started buying
the newspaper lately because there's a story about
some poor bastard who killed a bunch of people,
couldn't figure out why, and so turned himself in to
the President of the United States. In his words,
"his commanding officer." I've followed this story
like soap opera because I discovered that this guy
was in my second-grade class at Herbert Hoover
Elementary School. Although Roy Bonenkamp
never got in touch with his commander directly,
when it came time to burn the guy, a reporter from
the *Philadelphia Inquirer* remembered the military
reference and looked up his war record and discovered my old classmate had been a war hero and

LURP back in '65. The LURPS were the "long-range recon patrollers" who snuck out into the night to take VC camps and ambush columns of North Vietnamese before disappearing into the jungle where they lived. Lived, that is, until they took the "Big One." But Roy made it. Made it out to become a hero. The feature story made him a hero, and the President granted him clemency. He didn't accept and this morning they burned him.

The paper says they shaved the two spots on his head the night before. One next to his earlobe on the right side and the other in the center of the back of his head where there had been a soft spot when he was a baby. He wouldn't let them shave his legs—one final request. But they figured if they put enough K-Y jelly underneath the electrodes, they would have no problem frying him to death. They hadn't expected resistance or outcry during the crowded walk from the death tank to the backstage of the death room. And they didn't get any. The solitary chair, built out of the iron left over from the gallows which was used for the last time only fifty years before, was in readiness. They had torn down the gallows around the time his mother had been born.

I wrote him a letter, thinking maybe I could enter his life again and talk him into accepting clemency. I tried to commiserate. I told him we were old casualties now. Those out there who sit over morning coffee after a good game of squash have never heard of a LURP, and wouldn't be interested in Coptic crosses, 116th and Lenox or cassowary beaks—or they've decided to forget. He answered by sending me a picture of his back. Where the VC had sliced with their sickles were the undulating crevasses from twenty years of scar growth. It was the skin of another form of life process. But it was the backside of his head I would not have recognized as human without his sardonic comments annotating the different body parts—the mutilation was of a creative nature. The only responsive line in his communiqué referred to the fact that in reaching back beyond the barrier and into second grade he had plucked the image of a pretty little blonde girl who seemed self-referential at best from his damaged soul.

I don't know that I really care that they killed him or how. He wanted to die. I only mention it because in some way he is one of mine. He was learning to die not so long before I started.

I cab it as far as 96th and then get out to walk. My pace is with the cars though, and their power penetrates up into my groin and back out to their companions—they possess speed and the ability to push past boundaries. The turbulence of their swift shifting makes the dark air shimmer. With a pounding bass-line r&b cut in my head, and their urgent pace, I can imagine merging with the dark air. It's raining up the North Shore of the Long Island Sound. There are no stars out tonight and the mist is salty. Maybe if I'd gone to Roy Bonenkamp's cell yesterday morning I could have talked him into meeting me at Mikell's for just this one night, to share with me that sonic boom in our chests. Perhaps we could have danced. As a kid I remember him moving with a kind of grace. If we had just danced slowly, to a music of the jazz beat, if we had murmured to each other unintelligible things— merely as a nod to conversation—if we had held on to each other softly, gently, yet firmly enough to keep us both upright, we could have slipped into a mantra so subtle in its cry we might not have noticed when the rent out-priced us here. Maybe like speed-shifting, we wouldn't have even felt the rhythm of going into a higher gear, spiraling away into the outer darkness.

SPADE IN THE MINSTREL MASK

FOUR EBONY WOMEN IN WHITE GAUZE swoop down the front aisles at Radio City, tracked by strokes of stroboscopic light and accompanied by a bodiless orchestral sound. The girls press their hips out to individuals in the audience, solemn in their solo grind. They are regally abstracted, in waiting. The tempo picks up, and as if broken from a momentary embrace, they repeat to an inner rhythm steps that have traveled through time from the oldest culture.

Raised from below the stage is the figure of a man. Expectantly the dancers' faces turn childish in their honest awe. They raise their arms as they rush to the stage and form, just in time, an archway for Page as he steps off the platform. At that point the band sinks into a legendary r&b riff. Page exposes his dark brown chest covered by tiny coils of hair, his ghost-thin body melted into a suit of silver filigree finely sewn to the outline of his body yet creating the effect of vestigial chains. The thunder from the audience comes more from the pounding of hearts than even the sonorous applause. They love Page. They've loved him well and for a very long time. He never disappoints them. Rhinestones on his eyelids catch the lights, and the silver thread of his skintight bodysuit shines out to make him one great glowing moon surrounded by black. Black figures dressed in black playing guitar, timbals, bass, percussion—and he is the ebony god with a sex. A tall Abyssinian god whose thin, jagged body exists only to house his facile thoughts.

Page approaches the keyboard and firebombs explode in his wake as if the stage is mined. The sixty-foot color video screen hung behind the band shrieks to life with live footage of the riots in Jo'burg. Page's urban cool strut to the black fifteen-year-old Steinway is carefully side-tracked with the sweep of a red-hot and crimson-colored kleig that shoots its light onto the Southern white boy guitarist with the intensity of a bullet. He humps his microphone for apostrophe, he goes down on his guitar for sensuality, and then he plays the introductory riff, starting so high that when Page's ice-cool keyboard undermines the pitch, the synergistic reaction of their nervous energy meeting the mania of the crowd results in a suprahuman sound. Page pumps out rich arpeggios of sound with the glissando rush of a hot shot, shaking a hand in the air, Little Richard style, mimicking the ancestors and shrieking—*touch of death ain easy.*

Page Cook. Page Cook. Page Cook. His brother had been found shot dead in the face with one ear sliced off and said to be hanging around the neck of an Irish punk with a shaved head. Old days. Sirens blast onstage. Page Cook. Chants. Page had always been a little different. He was music. Synonymous in Bed-Stuy and Brownsville and Harlem and Hunt's Point was Page's name with music. His brother Van was out there first with a rep in the same places but for different things. Machine guns wipe the stage clean of sound and the video projects stills of stiffs in an Asian outpost in 1967. Same year Van came home. The stiffs are black or red white and blue. Page had played a harp first, then the keyboard. In fact, he played for his moms at Ebenezer every Sunday during his early days in a junior ace gang. But the day after his brother was iced, or so the story goes, he went mad. His brother stood for things— like being a man in no man's land. It was then that Page started speaking in code, the only way to understand him was to watch his hands—black long fingers speaking in signs. They said the cops found a white corpse with a black ear sewn on its forehead in the courtyard behind St. Vincent's and some say they've heard Page say it wasn't the gooks on some fuckmaster's hill who taught our white boys to make count necklaces out of VC ear. Page wears a black patch over his left ear and leans to the right when he plays. He moves so fast and freaks up so wild that he doesn't wait to see what's happening to him. That's the way it started. He locked himself in a room for days and played. He started hanging with other musicians. Clubs. He was only sixteen. The Disciples turned on him at first. His moms took him and his little sister out to Jackson Avenue in the Bronx. He taped himself every day after the late night sessions ending in the early morning hours: unique voicings expanded, unheard-of improvisations, cross chromatics like an acrostic puzzle foreign to conventional sounds, harmonies that had never ought to be. He would try it all out the next night if somebody let him pick up the chip. Van used to say the discipline for a musician's the same as it is for the white boy judges and senators.

Page finally got jobs in clubs on his name. Not pickup gigs. One of the first had been Said's. He did down dirty jobs for cash. Late night early morning. He brought it all home. Sent his sister Sheila to parochial school. He heard how a white boy dimed a player one night just to get the gig, but the w.b. never played again once the story hit the street. The rules were black man rules. White boy clubs didn't mean jack shit to Page Cook until he started comprehending jack. Van had explained money, power and discipline to Page. Page made a trip downtown to the Steve Paul Scene in '68, and when the keyboard man started throwing up, stinking with heroin death, Page picked up the shot. The rest is history.

Throughout the initial jam, bathed in a simple white spotlight, stands the bass player. Like the others, he is dressed in black, but his face is charred, his instrument is painted black, and a gigantic gallows frames him while a rope hangs down around his neck in mock execution. Page doesn't take to manufactured death, puncture wounds and punk twist. He games it. Page's flash on what he learned from Van about violence would go something like this. His eyes would wet. Always before a fight Van's eyes would tear in anticipation, the rage burrowing hot through his brain. His internal body adjusting for combat, Van would jig with his opponents to throw off their balance. The intoxication broke with the first blow and was replaced by finely controlled power. Then with ease and grace he would conquer. He saw himself as an urban artist, martial by necessity, tom-tom thick with the people who gave the texture to cities. He rejoiced in every thump and wail and he said he was here now and didn't have time to find out where his soul had been before and was going to next. He was violent and he was brutal, but he was smart and understood honor and loyalty. He understood too about waste. Van taught his little brother Page to respect the power of warfare but to learn to love something early. Page chose music, and with his music, he gets the payback.

And he does it with hard driving right-on-the-beat rhythm and blues. Does it with a three-chord blues progression and puts it in Mississippi and it's the country blues. Does a two bugs and a roach Earl Hooker and puts it in Chicago and it's urban blues. Does a four-part harmony and introduces Little Jimmy Scott falsetto and puts it on the street corner and it's the doo-wah rhythm and blues. Gives it a bass, a guitar, and a drum and puts it in Chuck Berry and it's rock and roll. Electrifies it and it's rock. Sweetens it with strings and it's pop. Talks it down and dirty street chant and it's rap. Bend a chord and invert a riff, music is the future through which he can avoid the past. Change the past. For Van.

Van used to say that if a man bears a child into Armageddon, better give the blood a dream. Page bought it. He found something to memory his brother with for not deferring the dream. The beat of rock and roll and power. Music was always there, even before Van died, but when Page found money and power he could promise his brother every night onstage that from now on when he sings about a boy on a beach like Rockaway, hand held high around the pretty little brownskin girl he takes into his arms behind the hard metal staircase in the urine stink of a project stairwell on 116th and Lenox, it will be he, Page, who is credited as creating the sound of the city with the power of that first shadowkiss. No more abc's of love figured and jammed out on a Harlem street corner by some sixteen-year-old singer who didn't have the power to say "this is mine" before he blasted away his mind on an OD as brutal as Johnny Ace's bullet.

The band sinks into a hard bass beat. Page rocks back and forth with his music, like a Balinese ecstasy dancer.

Spade, that spade

Did you hear about the plan
Runnin white as the Man
Got a mask for the task
And a soul like a casket

In the life, they say
And they know how to play

Cuz drama's the thing
Where life's got a deadly ring

Spade that spade
He's a spade in a mask
Minstrel mask is his identity
The mother's an obscenity

Predictability's not ability
Touch a death is the mobility
With a snake for a tongue
And a rap for a rep
The spade is a spade
And that's his suitability

Take your sisters off the street
Keep your mothers in the back room
The sucker's just a takeoff
Aimed at blood that can be ripped off

Turnin babies into pros
And childhood into doses
Motherfucker's got it comin
Like the Hawk when it be runnin

Hey Spade yo spade
You're a Spade in a mask
Minstrel mask is your identity

You're nothin but obscenity
Touch a death is my mobility

Master killer by definition
And I'm your competition.
That's death my Spade, death spade.

The shrieks from the little girls in the front row as
Page streaks across high stage acknowledge the rap.
Hand-held mike at his side, rigid arms dropping into
cool, alternating their position and lack of it—in the
way an African priest appears to fall in and out of
control yet always with his eyes on the sparrow. Control does not have the same meaning as it does for
the w.b.'s. *High-heeled sneakers* and *gangster leans*
were words tossed to the arena. His body is the geni-
tor, and therefore impervious to the language, to the
style set, to the new wave. He creates language, like
his brothers before him, he sets style and the only
wave is his wave. Those little girls are not puzzled in
the least by his grace and agility. His discipline. They
watch and they dance fast. And when his body goes
slow, it could be feeling hot. And when his body is
fast, it could be feeling cold. Any lack of distance,
any time he is thrown forward instead of back—back
into your body like dugie, like back into deep dugie—
it is Page gaming because it's about distance. The
floor chants, *He's so cool, he's icebox cool.*

At about 9:30 the door had opened to apartment 8-B in building number 305 of the Roosevelt projects and Sheila had walked in from the night, the smooth skin that covers the tender veins of her elbows and knees and neck and groin hardened and obscured by bruisings. She weighed about ninety-eight pounds.

Her eyes searched the apartment for a small radio, a Sony gadget coveted by her mother, anything small enough to dash out to the street market with. She had already taken all the items precious to the family which could bring in enough money on the street to buy sufficient doses to kill.

Bessie, asleep on the couch, the television's patter providing a familiar white noise for the book she had been reading, was not awakened when Sheila first entered the front room. Sheila knew her mother never slept very well and often spent her nights on the couch reading and watching the darkness weaken beyond the steel and glass project windows. It was Page who had dubbed their home "305" when they'd had to move into the projects, but it was Bessie who had refused to leave. At her age she wanted the freedom of familiarity. She didn't want the fancy addresses Page tried to talk her into. Maybe the people wouldn't talk to her there. Maybe she'd have to depend on other people driving her around. She wouldn't like that. So she stubbornly stayed on.

Bessie awakened with a start but Sheila didn't notice. Andra, who had come uptown before Page's gig to help her mother-in-law with Sheila's baby, heard the shuffling noises in the front room. She walked out from the baby's room, expecting to see Bessie preparing dinner. She gasped when she realized someone was pacing a few feet away from her in the dark. Hidden partially by Bessie's plants, whoever it was, was not Bessie because Bessie was on the couch. Suddenly Sheila spun around and out into the open space of the room, a knife the size of a gentlewoman's finger protruding from her tiny fist. The diminutive body perched erect and expectant upon her bony hips announced a staggering innocence. There was a pain going on between the two women both looked away from.

The richness of Sheila's chocolate skin and definition in the sensuous mouth crossed even the most parochial ethnic boundary of beauty. High African cheekbones and prominent heightened brow. A Semitic nose and the mouth of one of Botticelli's angels. Her birthright. Tonight she'd woven small ribbons into her dreads, as an afterthought—their tarnished life apparent—but nonetheless their presence, along with a filthy Gucci scarf Page had given her which she wore around her ankle, a declaration, saying, *Hey, I am, or, I was simply pretty!*

She has another birthright. There's a crimson blaze rush to being black gold. To rise to a dizzying height is to risk the free fall. The subsequent need is unappeasable and so the fix obvious. Andra's dark gray eyes rimmed with a brown darker than the hue of her brunette hair resonate with the same disjunction as her friend.

When Andra glanced again at her mother-in-law, she saw that Bessie was not asleep. Sheila had already folded the knife away and walked into the kitchen. Bessie held her finger up to her lips to signal Andra's silence.

Andra followed Sheila.

"You got some juice?"

"No Sheila, there's only a little orange left and it's for the baby. Let me give you some milk."

"Yeah. Okay. Where's Page? He ain't here?"

"He's got a gig at Radio City tonight. I gotta meet him later. Wanna come? That why you're here?"

Sheila and her brother loved each other unconditionally. Nothing either could do in life would threaten their bond.

"Don't make me no nevermind. Where's my baby?"

"In your room."

"You stayin there?"

"I was playing with the baby. Till I leave for downtown. Is that OK?"

"Of course. I mean, thanks."

Suddenly Bessie was in the kitchen doorway behind Sheila, holding the knife she always slept with. Everyone was used to seeing her wield it. She'd never stuck anyone, yet her unpredictability was as complete as her daughter's. She could strike or withdraw.

Sheila flipped out her little cut-off stiletto and slumped coldly against the refrigerator, a beat as rational as the rule of the wild thumping from her eyes. You come for me—I go for you. No family. No mothers here.

"Bessie, don't make a scene. I'm leaving."

"And what're you leaving with this time? Spreading your junkie-ass germs in my house. You already got our money, you want our flesh to bring back yours?"

The words stung the quiet. Each person waited, watching with despair as the moment developed, until the horrible silent choking began. Bessie dropped the knife and sobbed tearlessly. Her body had been fed only by gin that day. Sheila finished her milk, whisked the blade back into its husk and strode out of the kitchen. She didn't go back to see her baby. She pulled out a pack of Salems and left two on her mother's gray pillowcase stuffed into the corner of the couch. She had borrowed a lot of cigarette money from her mother over the years.

As soon as the door slammed shut, Bessie opened the gin bottle and drank from the mouth. Andra sat at the kitchen table and stared out the window onto the project playing ground. Sheila used to sit at the small aluminum table for hours, gazing indifferently out the window. Then when the monkey claws dug flesh and she couldn't stand it any longer, she would nonchalantly put on her red corduroy jacket designed by a French millionaire and slip out the door into the night as if she were going to Met Food for Salems. The waiting would begin. One month, sometimes two or three and finally Page would meet her in the street after days of cruising Harlem praying for a glimpse. But he wouldn't bring her home if she didn't want to come. He respected the deal. She'd take some money for food and he wouldn't tell Bessie. Bessie had already started using the bottle as a way of going back in spirit to that place before drugs and street time.

The playground was black in the late-summer final twilight hour. The benches Bessie sat on during the day were abandoned and the damp mud earth around them shone like a carpet from the reflected light of the emerging moon. Andra saw Sheila cross the shining mud to the sidewalk in front of the opposite building and stop. Sheila looked back at the steps into her street-scarred lobby and then glanced up to the eighth floor where Andra stood. Sheila didn't wave. The hesitation was enough. She drifted over the paths of her childhood, threading her way through the red brick buildings to Lafayette Avenue, where she slid into a green Pinto waiting for her on the corner.

There's this sound. It's soft like the excitement of hot weather, summer nights. Andra hears it as she drives back into the city to meet Page at Radio City. Page knows the sound. The lights of the bodega twinkling long after closing time, its children shirking the bedtime ritual to squeal along the storefront in celebration of this occasional freedom. A girl swaying, hips one way, arms the other, to this sound, on a stoop up on Jackson Avenue. It reminds Andra of a light summer sundress. Red. One Bessie had given her. She remembers carrying the baby across the street to the liquor store to find her mother-in-law, the mother's pretty light brown skin flushed and spotted from too much gin and too many arguments. Andra knows the baby as her sister or other close relation. The baby's top lip is a touch larger than the lower one and so pulls her mouth into a little bow-pout. Beads of perspiration on her forehead and in the crease down the middle of her tiny chest don't bother her as she sighs an adult, disinterested sigh. Little ringlets of soft brown hair are matted to her tiny caramel cheeks. She had been born a junkie. Her first struggle to begin life had been compounded by one to stay alive. But she is like Andra and Sheila and Bessie—quiet, waiting for the commotion to subside, given to sudden bursts of joy.

When the call is picked up in the sound booth by Page's head roadie, he transfers it to a back-stage extension where the road manager stands ready. Andra has stopped at the corner of 138th and Lenox Avenue on her way down to Page and thinks maybe she ought to stay uptown and look for Sheila. She tells the road manager she needs Page and decides when she discovers he's so near the end of the first act of his set that she will hold on. Hearing him in the background singing "Spade" with a tone she recognizes as one of cold immacu-late hatred, she drops into the reverie that has in-formed every day of her third decade.

Sheila and Andra had been running buddies long before Andra ever met Page. She'd heard about him and his brother's rep, but as a Catholic schoolgirl living in the Bronx, she had led a very protected life. It was with Sheila she had donned her sling-backed red halter top and leather miniskirt in prepa-ration for the first time they hung at Said's. On the way to Said's that long-ago night, Andra and Sheila had passed 46th Street and the Nightstalk Pussy Club where the sounds steaming from the interior matched the stick on the inside of the glass fish tanks that held the naked girls. Dark-haired, big-eyed sixteen-year-old girls breaking hearts, revealing nothing of themselves as they lay glued to alien textures. Sheila and Andra knew they would never end here. Their eyes were on the sparrow, which soared up where few black girls had been—where the air was thin and there was no one else to hold on to. Desire can overcome the vertigo up there, but with the vertigo is the compulsion to jump, a compulsion impelled more by the call of emptiness than a natural fear.

After most of Sheila's girlfriends had been eaten up *in the life*, she stood alone at the precipice. They beckoned to her demanding that she renounce the sparrow. Plunder the gold. The quavery tremolo in Billie Holiday's voice, when she was on top, was a hesitation about all that she'd been taught to believe was her destiny. *God bless the child who's got her own.* Billie didn't get hers soon enough. In that hesitation there is a weakness. And who would not sound weak when facing the superior strength of a destiny.

And so as the panic seeped in after Van's murder, in the flush of hot death, Sheila had drawn away from Andra and Page. The first time Andra and Page knew for certain what was going down was when they'd had to bring Sheila in on a gurney made of Page's jacket from his gang days. The pieces of red wrapping paper threaded to the Christmas gift ribbon tying Sheila's hands gleamed with an iridescence that forced Page to remember other things, a place that time had killed. Page had started to cry, his memory slipping back to a crisp Christmas morning innocent of destinies. He had shivered in the hallway of the hospital, his thin T-shirt not protection enough against the faintness of Sheila's heartbeats. Pain's a slight motherword. Page had stood on the sight side of a two-way glass connecting the now-familiar cold tanks for detox. In the next room Sheila sat strapped in a purple gown with sleeves the length of three wraps about her skinny body, a cigarette loosely suspended between her ruby brown lips. Page walked into the tile-padded room and flicked the ash of his sister's cigarette. Page had always called her Ruby after her fine full lips. He told their mother that night about the deafening commotion and her child.

"What's happening baby?"

Andra jumps at the sound of Page's voice. Like a bird in flight when first hit, before the knowledge and the fall, she is electrified only by the sensation.

"Sheila. She was home. I'm worried. I don't..."

"Tell me."

"She was only home for a minute, but she was walking funny. Like her bones aren't right. I'm on my way downtown, but I thought maybe I should stop at Said's. See if anyone knows where she is."

"Meet me here. We'll go together. Twenty minutes."

Andra hangs up the phone and stares at the defaced phone booth smelling of junkie urine. She thinks about Page and the multi-million-dollar concert and sees Sheila and the stink of drug death. She starts the car at '38th and roars down Lenox, stopping at Said's anyway. Said's is the joint. She parks in the back where there are a few spots saved for the regulars. Your license number is your membership in the club. All kinds of clubs in the world. It's a closed set. Private. Van used to say that Harlem's his bitch and Said's his teacher.

Andra's not a member, but the minute she walks in, the crowds part to let her pass. They don't like that she's here without Page, but nevertheless she's Page Cook's woman. A young man Andra knows from Sheila, but only in passing—Kenny—approaches her. Something is wrong tonight. She senses it. Kenny peers at her through blazing eyes set deep into his face. Kenny's a high roller. Has been since he was eight. He makes it with the high, loves the high and jostles it freely in his veins. Loves the high of the spike itself. He puts everything inside. They say he cuts holes in his shoulder to play with the air bubbles he shoots into his arm. He's been lured inexorably by the emptiness that has caught his homeboys, and right now he reads scared. Kenny says:

"I know where she's headed."

"Where?"

"Page."

"What's wrong with her. You been with her?"

"I took care of her, but she seemed sick. She was in the wind before I could stop her."

With her eyes Andra cuts Kenny the nod out to her car. The crowd watches. Kenny's got a rep too. Andra appreciates this fact. He holds his high. He doesn't take orders. He gives them. He's been dealing since he was eight. He makes his drug money legit. He's never stolen a dime and everyone knows it. That makes him proud. But neither does he want to go down as the dude who did Page Cook's sister the final round. He pretends to want to go find Sheila.

"Did she use here?"

"No. She copped and slammed."

"So you don't know what stuff made her sick—not yours?"

Kenny figures to be honest here. "I don't know." Andra drives him across the border into midtown. Across 110th Street. They both know how to deal a safe house. Andra sweeps the streets around Radio City then jumps out of the car at the back-stage door. Big Beau is there—Page's main man—waiting for her. Beau is part African American, part Thai, and all artist. His form is Burmese. He takes the car while Andra and Kenny enter the side door, Andra flashing passes. When she hits the stairs, Kenny stumbles behind her, feeling sick. He needs a hit. Andra knows the way to Page's room and most of the security recognize her. She drags Kenny after her now. She wants to get there fast. When they reach the second floor Andra turns down toward the green room. She's stopped by a fleet of security. Sonny Goldman stands just behind the pack. Andra's known Sonny for years. He promotes all of Page's New York gigs. He steps through the wall of flesh and grabs her hand. Sonny asks:

"Who's the waste-out with you?"

"A friend. Let him follow."

Andra has a tight grip on Kenny's arm. He doesn't seem to mind. He's jigging with something in his pocket. She doesn't miss a beat as she waves to the punk and glitter babies decorating the metal stair-well with flash, waiting for the band. Sonny keeps it up:

"What happened to you tonight? I thought you wanted to make the show."

"I did."

Andra doesn't pursue the explanation. She doesn't owe one to anybody.

"I'll take you to Page's room."

"You got another room you can lock?"

"Down the hall."

"I got some talkin to do with this sorry excuse for living. But first I need to squat with Page. Can you cut me some time and privacy?"

Sonny takes Andra and Kenny past Page's chambers, through a locker room to a small cell with a desk, a chair and a light bulb hanging from the ceiling. Andra turns to Kenny, sits him in the chair and starts to walk. Kenny summons the energy for language.

"What the fuck ya doin?"

"I'm doin what shoulda been done to you a long time ago. Long time before you met Sheila."

"What's that?"

"Lockin you up. But you're gonna help me find Sheila."

Andra slams the door and nods curtly for Sonny to lock it. He doesn't ask any questions. Andra's squeeze brings him at least two hundred thousand a year every year.

"Take me to Page."

Backstage, a scene reminiscent of the ritualized boxing match where deification of the master is common is taking shape: thunderous applause explodes past the phalanx of men commencing to move, cross-armed and martial, as escort to Page. When Page passes Andra in the darkened space behind the stage curtain, he grabs her. He touches her shoulder and drops his hand down her back. Still vibrating from the show, his touch carries the gentle hiss from the wind of the hawk. She leans into him. They are solid. And with the barely cradle-broken shadow girls following like little birds at Cinderella's Ball, this couple touched momentarily by fairy tale is ushered back to Page's quarters.

Andra drops onto the green couch next to the buckets of roses set up on three-tier steps. Page hunches over the small Wurlitzer perpendicular to the couch, beating out a harmony against a three-chord pump. He can't come down yet. The sounds are hammering his brain.

"What's good, baby?"

"I told you. Sheila."

"We'll go now. Let me get straight first."

Page diddles a melody that sinks into Andra's heart. Andra doesn't tell Page the whole deal. She's anxious about Kenny locked up in the room down the hall. She's distracted by the time that is passing. Page stands up suddenly and comes over to Andra from behind. Uncharacteristically he lays his arm across his wife's breast and smothers his face in her hair. His embrace is for dear life. Andra feels his thin Abyssinian nose and ashy brown skin scrape out a raw in her she had tried to forget was there.

Page pulls himself up from the comfort of his wife's hair. Her dark hair smells of muguet—lily of the valley. He turns off the lights and returns to Andra's warm body. With the flat of his hand he holds her just in the center of her buttocks. Pressing. She asks him:

"The set was good?"

"I'm still feelin it."

The knock at the door simply unsettles Page. He has a slight sense of unease. Andra however catapults from the couch, the image of Kenny as she left him plaguing her.

Page pulls her back, murmuring, "Don't answer it yet. Just take it easy. For a minute. We'll find Sheila." Then, as his own edginess coalesces: "Where's Ma?"

"Nothing to worry about there."

"Yeah." He relaxes.

The knocks grow louder and Andra stiffens with rising fear as she listens to the hollow voices from the hallway. She thinks she hears Sonny mention Sheila's name. She blurts out:

"Page, we gotta open the door."

Page hears the dry panic in his wife's voice and is halfway to the door by the time Andra leaps from the couch. Sonny and the roadies are crowded in the narrow, brightly lit hallway outside Page's dressing room. When the door flies open Page appears in technicolor against the dark, still dressed in silver lamé, the sweat of his body sparkling in the glare. Sonny comes forward as if emissary from the line of concerned faces and, without saying a word, leads Page down to the room where Andra and he had locked up Kenny less than a half hour ago.

Sonny stutters, "I saw your sister here. Then I saw the guy Andra and I locked up. He must have gotten out and found your sister because now I think they're back in the locked room together."

Page whips around and screams Andra, draining her of her high color. He doesn't know what Sonny is talking about. He had told Andra to come directly to the gig. Page doesn't listen further. He grabs the hand of Beau, his old companion and head security artist, and glances to the door. They smash into it on the dime. The door buckles and there is a shout from inside. Beau hammers the door with his powerfully trained foot and Page splinters the door frame by blasting the door off its hinges with the side of his left hand.

Kenny is standing over Page's sister. He has shot Sheila with a needle he shaped with the filaments from the naked overhead bulb. Coldly, without missing a beat, Page grabs Beau's nine-millimeter

Browning filled with fourteen-shot hollow points and shoots Kenny flat in the chest. Kenny falls back against a wall and collapses on Sheila's body. Page kicks Kenny out of the way. His sister is unconscious. He leans over and plucks her from the stunned silence playing in the crowd. Andra holds Sheila's head as Page carries her from the room. She directs Sonny to call an ambulance. One of the roadies crouches over Kenny. He's alive. Page isn't thinking about Kenny. He isn't even thinking about Andra. Holding his sister as he runs down the cement steps of the backstage staircase, Page evokes the image of the plaster pietà that used to sit on Sheila's bedroom dresser. He used to take the stairs in the projects fast. With skill. Street skill. From home.

One night Page and his little Ruby had stayed up late together and played the magic game. If Page made it across 110th Street, what would he buy for Ruby? And if Ruby did, what did Page want? Ruby had wanted a chifforobe like the one she and Page used to keep their clothes in back on Jackson Avenue. It was the prettiest piece of furniture they owned in those days; a scene of cherubs had been painted on with white clouds and happy faces. Page had wanted to be a star.

A limo driven by an off-duty New York City cop is waiting out front for Page. He bears Sheila to the car. Andra slides in next to him. Page doesn't speak. Whatever skills he has ever developed have now failed him. The vertigo hits heavy. Ambulances and cop cars shriek in the night shroud. They are distant sounds but they close in on him and jerk him back when, after what seems like seconds, the limousine pulls up in front of the hospital.

Page does not release his sister from his arms even as he crosses the threshold of the hospital emergency room. He can feel her life still in her. The doctors and nurses rush him. A blur of white. They seem to form an archway for him as he steps into their landscape. Andra whispers to him, *let go*. He cannot. He's keeping Ruby's life inside her. He hears someone behind him say *Isn't that Page Cook?* Page staggers. He has not taken off his stage clothes and there are makeup smears on his face and around his eyes. He is oddly not out of place in this emergency room where the war paint of drama is an all-times thing. He thinks he hears that same person shout *Who's the spade in the minstrel mask?* Page turns and sees that there is a man in blue. More than one. One of them yells that Page Cook's junkie sister spiked out at the Radio City gig and Page Cook jammed the guy who spiked her. Right there. Front and center.

Andra pries Page's fingers from Sheila's little-sister-help-me-please body, carefully and tenderly. *Ruby will be okay if you just let the doctors help her.*

What had Kenny wanted when he played the magic game? What answer would Kenny's brothers and sisters give Page—if anyone was still alive to repeat Kenny's request?

Page's eyes tear. Like the old days with Van. As if his body were adjusting for combat. This time it is he who is the aggressor. The ebony god. But Page is only a man in the mask of the warrior. Fighting from a position of superior strength is not warrior ethic. Nine-millimeter Brownings are about killing, not honor.

He swats at a sting in his ear, like a hiss, and then he notices that his wife is speaking. Through the steam he hears her say that the doctors are trying to tell them it is time to call Bessie. The fighting is at an end. They must call Bessie now. Tell her where her children are. Tell the mothers where their children are—as if they didn't fear. They would have to call and tell her though...the commotion out there is so deafening, she might not hear. The commotion won't cease, so they might not hear. The mothers.

THE SHOPPER

I T ISN'T AS IF THE DARK ROOM BOTHERS HER; there is a lightbulb she can turn on in the closet if she needs to. When Eddie brought her home tonight he asked if she wanted to go to the hospital. The pains were just dull though, and he being a cop and all, he might try to take it away from her.

He isn't a bad guy—Eddie. The rest of them always tried to move her along, away from the shops on the main floor of the mall. They let a lot of the hustlers be busy there, but money talks and yata yata, they made her walk. She was never doing anything special. She'd just stand in front of, like, Benetton and Footloose. They had Reeboks in Footloose. She had wanted Reeboks for four years. She saw them on all the girls in Portland.

The girls would walk briskly along the waterfront in neat-fitted tan skirts and white blouses unbuttoned just by one so that a pearl necklace could show coyly underneath, next to the skin, without being sexy. They had all probably been cheergirls when they were in high school. Now they went to interesting jobs, like in art galleries on Fore Street, or chic nouvelle stores that carried Perry Ellis, in the old section of Portland, down by the port, where all the developers were busy restoring the old buildings. These girls would enter into their nice warm shops filled with soap scents, like Covent Garden on Exchange Street between Spring and Pleasant, and there each girl would sit on a little wooden stool after unwrapping her teal sweater tied around her shoulders, and slip off her Reeboks she had walked to work in, and slide smoothly into a pair of Magli sling-backs, her sleek heels shining through the fine-textured hosiery bought at Fogal. From looking into the windows of Amaryllis and Alfiero's where they imported Italian sweaters and pants and fabrics she loved to touch, she had learned all about clothes, even what they called couture. She bought her pair of Reeboks in the spring of '95.

Eddie's work starts at eleven at night, so she gears her hours to his shift. She's been doing the mall nighttime hours and, until recently, the Old Port by day. The last place on Exchange Street that had let her in was Serendipity, where they caught her with ten angora sweaters in the fitting room. She told them that she was trying them all on to see which colors were best suited for her tan skirt she'd left at home. A very sweet-faced girl helped her unbutton the purple sweater she had covered the pistachio-colored pullover with, that she wore over a pink cashmere she had initially tried on over her black bra from Victoria's Secret. It wasn't that she ever stole anything, because she didn't ever do things like that, but she guessed they thought she might steal something or make a scene or, now, maybe even get something dirty. But what with the window shopping, she could still keep up on all the latest styles and trash lingo.

The thing about window shopping is that all the best stuff is in the window anyway. One time she had seen a mannequin holding a placard that said: "Buy by the nanosecond." She'd liked that word. Nanosecond. She went to the public library in Monument Square and found out it was a real word. Her mind spiraled into a dark cavern as she tried to imagine the length of time it took to be a nanosecond.

Sure she scores easier this time of night too. But even Pedlar flees once the buy is made. She thinks maybe he put a button man on her once. She figures he might be a cop and she will have to move on soon from this place. Eddie is nice but he is still a cop too. And furthermore she doesn't go out on wet nights in her Reeboks.

The dull pain must be her sign. She is ready. She's heard about boiling water from when her mother took her to see *Gone with the Wind*. She draws the rusty scissors across the gas flame—there is no pot to boil the water in—and opens up the case of razor blades she's bought for the occasion. She carefully parses out the articles from her brown bag. Thread. Needles in a little silver pack. Plum fingernail polish that matches her plum lipstick she bought last week. Clamps for pulling a lobster out of a pot once it turns red.

A week earlier she had cut the seat out of a chair to offer the baby a birth space. She'd read something about these birth seats when she was hanging outside Marty's News in Monument Square.

She places the chair in the closet and turns on the light. She squats for a minute in the corner behind her bed, watching the altar she has made of the chair with the one light in the room shining down upon it, making it glow. She feels its woodenness. She'd heard the wood gasp when she cut the hole for the birthing space. She hears things. She hears her Reeboks breathing in the closet. They are placed next to the straightened coat hanger across from her chair. She anticipates the ache she will feel when the hanger is inserted inside the extended lips of her vagina.

It isn't just her personal possessions that she hears. She hears the teal of the girls' sweaters. And she has heard red. It sometimes occurs to her that she is mad. She hears maverick cells depart from a healthy site and she'd heard the bloody storm when her mother's spirit rose up to fight her illness. She had heard the terrible chasm on her mother's last good day, and she had heard the slight wind surge before she killed the father of this child. This wouldn't be an easy birth she'd heard.

She'd killed the big hairy Cajun who'd done her in a parking lot in one of the streets off the downtown park in Lewiston. She'd wandered over to Lewiston from Portland for the weekend of the Cajun Music Festival the second week in August. She'd read about it in the little digest the chamber of commerce in each town puts out and then sends to all the public libraries in each state. She had always loved music, and the eerie wild incantations of Cajun music were reminiscent of a primordial sound she associated with gypsies and Bohemia. She had the high and wide cheekbones of a Slav, but her eyes were dark and almond shaped like a gypsy renegade of that heritage, and her skin had the olive tones of the Mediterranean.

The Cajun was about six four and weighed over 250. She could hear the violence in his hands, which she disliked but was compelled by; and she had seen with her own eyes how on Sunday morning, early, the Cajun women would be walking Delacroix Street with black eyes and sexy dark hose. So when the Cajun started beating on her she pulled a knife. She plunged it into his belly when he wouldn't stop. She always kept the knife strapped underneath her right sock like an ankle bracelet. She flipped it out with some dexterity and in a movement that did not surprise her, jammed it into the Cajun's gut. He stopped. Perplexed at first. Then he grabbed at the knife in its soft throbbing wound and wailed like a banshee. She stepped back, not inappropriately, and turned on her heel to leave. She felt like one of the cheergirls. They used words like totally, definitely, completely and absolutely. They were so sure of what they thought and said and did. Certitude. Nanoseconds. She had her Reeboks on, so when she turned on her heel they squeaked ever so slightly.

She knew she hadn't killed him. The stomach is a pretty safe place to stick somebody even though it's a blood pumper. It stops a man in his tracks but doesn't do too much damage, especially when the target is so big and fat. She'd laughed all the way home. Maybe a little hysterically. She'd knifed a couple other people, but it always upset her. She wasn't a bitter person. She liked other people just fine and usually understood their ways. She wasn't mean or violent. But she didn't take shit either. She couldn't. Otherwise she'd be dead.

Later when she read about this big fat Cajun guy they found dead in a parking lot in Lewiston the day after the Cajun Music Festival, she couldn't believe the article might involve anyone she could know. But as she thought, and as time went by, she felt a little differently. She lost her concentration. Her focus. Used to be that she would get up of a morning and plan her rounds. She'd wash her hair and select a perfect nail polish for the day, clean the polish from the day before and begin anew under the light of the oncoming day. Up until this year she'd had a couple of outfits she could mix and match with different belts and imitation Hermés scarves so that by the time she left her little room above Jack Fastener's Automotive Store on Brackett, she looked more than a little presentable.

She had loved going to the Portland library. Going there was a centerpiece event in her day. They never turned her away. Even now. She had a card. She'd applied for the card over two years ago. She had gotten dressed up in a skirt and blouse. Her legs were bruised, not from anything special, just from living and stuff, but most people who went to libraries didn't have that many bruises all over them, so she got very dark hose and nobody noticed. She didn't have her Reeboks then, so she wore whatever shoes she had. Shoes were expensive. She figured that the people at the library were so nice to her because it was run by the government for the public and she was part of the public; they were trained not to be upset if she didn't look exactly right. She liked the government for that, and for other things too. She was so comfortable at the library, she'd just breeze right in no matter what she had on—if she needed to look up a word or finish a piece in the paper she'd started at Marty's News before Marty's son shooed her away.

But she knew she'd deteriorated since the Cajun. Not that she hadn't had some problems before that. But it was her red hair that had always shocked people. It was beautiful. And she kept it clean. It glistened in the sun in the summer and the tourists would buy the little pins she made out of clover she picked in front of the state house, because they thought she was only some kind of hippie. Now it was matted. She'd tried the curly look last summer and started using mousse, but once everything got so confusing it was hard to find the time to comb the mousse out. It was just too much. So the tangles got more mangled and she just let them be. She pretty much lived in the same dress and coat every day, too.

When she'd found out about the baby, she'd gone to Porteus, because it was such a conservative department store, and picked out a nice dress and coat for the winter that were big enough to grow with her. They'd been expensive, but she couldn't go walking around in something cheap at this time in her life. They were made by Pendleton, an old American company she'd read about, that made the kind of clothes she should be wearing at this time. She bought Porsche sunglasses in the second-hand store so she wouldn't strain her eyes now, but passed up the used Peugeot bassinet, promising herself that when the baby was born she'd buy new things. She'd buy everything later when there was more money. But she did record her name in the bridal registry at Porteus, in case someone thought to buy her anything in the meantime, like the crystal and china her child should one day inherit.

She begged that winter. It was hard work. And she gave away a lot of her sort of frivolous clothes to Goodwill. She had to be sensible now. If the hotels or restaurants would have let her waitress she would have been overjoyed to go inside and work, but no one had hired her since 1994 when she worked as a stock girl in a wine and cheese store. They were nice people there. But she must have acted a little weird, because when they fired her they told her how much they liked her and they gave her four weeks' pay and tried to be really nice. Except when she returned to hang out a bit, they didn't really want to talk to her. She was used to people being like that though. And she didn't hate anybody for it. But one thing was for sure. Nobody could beat on her.

She had always thought she was probably very beautiful. There were these high sleek cheekbones, like all the models wanted, and then the dark watery eyes that sounded like fire and, last, there was the red hair. None of these things usually were found together. They were each beautiful, each thing, and the combination should have made everyone want to care for her. Take care of her. But it hadn't worked out that way. She stared at her face every day in the mirror. Sometimes endlessly. If she liked herself well enough, that would be good enough.

When Eddie saw her at the mall tonight, she was swaying like a drunk. Her hair didn't look so beautiful. He thought he had to bring her home because she was high or something worse. He was nice to her and never beat on her. He'd seen her for the first time way back when her red hair was still squeaky clean and shiny. She had told him how when she was a child in the Midwest she had tap-danced at the state fair for the crippled children. That her mother had taken her around to all the crippled children's hospitals in Iowa and Illinois to tap-dance for the little children who couldn't walk so good.

She goes to the tiny gas stove and grasps the scissors and razor blades and then moves to the chair in the closet. She sits for several moments under the spot of light, as if paralyzed by the weight of her decision, and then slowly, beginning at that point between the breasts where the sternum starts, she imagines making an incision. She will have to drive the sharpened razor blade in more deeply as she moves downward, ending just below the curve of her ripe belly. Once there, she will peek into her belly. She will lean forward like a throwaway rag doll, and if she cannot see the baby yet, she will gouge ever deeper into the cavity with the swipe of the razor.

As preparation, she inserts her own fingers deep inside her vagina. Her discomfort is putting her near a place she never imagined. Flipping her finger around, she can touch the crown of the baby which seems closer to her natural opening than she expected. She discards the scissors but keeps them alongside the chair, and with what she believes to be surgical precision, she separates the skin of her labia with her razor. Pain thunders in her ears. She needs to cradle the little baby in her arms. She gives a tug, anxious. She hears the baby's blood babbling through its healthy body. Like a boxer, alone in his spotlight, knowing that only he can summon up the blow so exquisite that events will alter and course his way, she believes that only alone and by following her instincts will she be able to give this baby a life. Immaculately alone, she can untwist all that has led up to what is now. And like that boxer, she has so prepared for the pain that, when it comes, she does not feel it. She sees a deep purple and knows absolutely and with certitude that as two, she and her child will start again.

Elated, she sits straight up and pushes down with her inner muscles. A white light flashes across her forehead and she sees Eddie standing in front of her with a complete layette for the baby. He displays the little articles of clothing resplendently across the bed, and there, sparkling in the corner, is a glistening white bassinet. A handmade quilt lies nestled inside, awaiting the infant. She is bedazzled. She pushes down hard and sticks her fingers underneath her. She thinks she can feel the head now outside of her body. She looks up to tell Eddie, but he has disappeared; only the clothing and bassinet remain.

There is a knocking at the door. Instinctively she reaches down for her stiletto. As she bends over, the baby's body moves forward and down. She thinks it is a boy. With one hand she clutches the crown and with the other she prepares to defend.

She recognizes Eddie's voice outside, but does not relax or trust. There might be someone with him.

Inside her concentration she believes she hears the baby slip out. They must be still connected. On her knees atop the bed she faces the door with her stiletto and hollers.

Eddie slams the door in then and she senses his alarm and that it is for her, not against her. She collapses into the baby garments on the bed as they join to comfort her. She knows that the tiny boy must have red hair for he sounds like an echo of that color. She'll buy him Reeboks as soon as she feels like shopping.

Eddie lifts them both from the bed and carries them gently. She relaxes because Eddie does not try to part her from her son. A fire she heard in the chasm when her mother died licks at her heel and she fears her strength for the first time. The light is so daunting that she closes her eyes. A shimmer of her mother arises in the glare. Finally its peculiarities reach her. She could lean down and touch her mother's brow. She wonders if her son can hear the roaring fire it takes to make the light brilliant. The stains of her life, so vivid now in the glow of the fire, threaten to blunt her force in this all-important nanosecond.

She remembers the night she had watched some puny club fighter come from behind in the eighth round to clobber his Goliath. She'd learned about winning from the boy-sports the cheergirls watched from the sidelines. It was simple. You couldn't give up, even if you didn't have your stiletto on you.

She concentrates, holding the baby's head, feeling a heartbeat. It's a struggle. The light pounds in her ears. But it carries her too. She recalls how the sports boys would say it's not over till it's over.

Sensing her arrival at a new location that smells antiseptic, she prepares to be separated from her infant. She reminds herself of the certitude of separation. She'd gone through it with her own mother. And with that thought a bewildering rush of visions replaces the fire. A boy stands beautiful, straight backed and red haired, wearing Reeboks and an authentic Ferragamo scarf decorated with tigers. She can see that it is her son—so new to the very air he breathes apart from her for the first time— keeping her tight in the light, away from the flames. His hair curls into smiles and his lean frame tells her of energy and intent. He has her wide cheekbones and dark eyes. She imagines he will shop at the stores run by the cheergirls and she knows no one will ever relegate him to the windows on the street side. She knows that for certain. Absolutely.

THE TRYST

THIS NIGHT HE WALKS UP TO WHERE SHE SITS. He bends down and kisses her breast, covering her nipple with his wet mouth. She is wearing a crisp white cotton blouse and the darkness his mouth makes sinks through her bra to the point her nipple has become. She looks down, intrigued, while he slides into the bench next to her. They don't speak. An island reggae band dominates the stage with a presence that transforms the club into a Jamaican countryside at night. Children in shared beds, soft inland breezes meeting the coos of night animals and the spicy aroma of earthy *ganja* accompanying the low murmur of male voices. The drone picks up and abates, up and back in the rhythm of patois, a rhythm that matches the tropical waves in the afternoon, an excitable lyrical language that can easily become music, being already of that nature. Gylan looks straight ahead as he slips his hand under Jane's skirt. She lifts her legs slightly to fold his fingers into her body. She doesn't wear underwear, and tonight she has worn the bra as an enticement. He sticks his fingers deep inside her. She begins to sway with the music, never glancing at him and humming along to the lyric— *I'd strike the sun if it struck me.*

She is beautiful. She has been to many places. That is her job. She makes a breezy animal noise. She sways with the music, moving on his tense palm. He leans over and says only if you love me. Words have the meaning she gives them. She hums words heavy with city madness. The people she speaks of bruise what bruises them and from the nuance in her words it is clear she does not bother with dreams anymore. She says she's a rambler playing out the riddle of calm turbulence. She speaks in riddles. When she touches the end of a rainbow her fingertips bend the colors back into what rains on gypsy streets, that place which houses every creature whose time is dusk and whose half-life jumps past midnight. Gylan knows she's some place where music has replaced the inadequacy of words, but he doesn't care. If it's crazy he's dealing with, he's been there—her gestures are grand. She lives on a large scale. Up where the gods and poets game. Her beauty is high-boned yet funky. Her lips are full like a Semite and her eyes span other worlds. The hope is that if someone can catch the light there for a minute, he will see what she sees.

Someone across the club waves. She pretends not to see.

"You been here before?" Gylan asks by rote. The play.

"No."

He knows otherwise. But he'll play. She wears a lion's mane of hair around eyes that burn life into something he doesn't know about. Something that has nothing to do with happiness or contentment, but is vivid in a way that the night sky is when comets collide out of an imperative no more human than the electrifying death of their wake.

"What'll ya drink Miss?" The bartender looks into Gylan's face as he speaks to Jane. She just needs something to take the edge off.

"A beer please."

She never drinks beer. The bartender winks at Gylan. He knows the game too.

"We have Michelob, Heineken and Coors on tap."

"What's he drinking? I'll have whatever he's drinking." She thumbs Gylan.

Gylan touches her knee.

"Heineken," he says.

Gylan keeps watching her. Good. She can feel her strength flowing back.

"Who's the singer?" she says.

The fingers on his right hand are stained with tobacco. The singer is a dwarf.

"Her name is Olive."

"That's a dreadful name."

He takes a sip from his beer and looks out to Olive. He is about six foot. Jane imagines that Gylan skewers the midget woman on his cock like a cork-screw.

"She's Basque."

"I know."

"How do you know?"

"There's an announcement right behind her at the piano."

"It says she's Basque?"

"Why not?"

Gylan looks quickly and very softly he asks Jane to stop the game and come home with him. His voice comes out low and young and handsome. She wants to fuck his voice.

"Does anyone call you by any other name, Jane?"

"Do you?" She asks the question as softly as he has, and looks at his hands. They are exquisite.

"Do you want to go home with me?" Gylan inquires obliquely.

"Are you picking me up?"

"No, I'm asking you to come home with me." This time he is direct.

"Do you cost money otherwise?"

"No—blood."

His head rocks up and down with laughter then. The laugh explodes past his teeth untamed—and then it stops. It doesn't match his stare. She wants to go home. She's had enough of this outing.

"The pain is better now," she says.

"How can pain be better?"

"Don't mean it that way."

"How do you know how I mean it?"

"Fuck you."

"Fuck you."

"You're of a certain age, aren't you?"

"War-age. That what you mean?" He smiles. Silence.

"It's late. You can take me home."

"We'll miss the traffic."

"Friction. Friction. Traffic of the soul. You'll hit it no matter the late hour."

Gylan bends down and kisses her thigh. The mood is changed. There is a place she lives. It is inside. Deep inside and it takes over sometimes, still and white. When she sits and drinks her tea, mornings, she looks out a window to the green she is surrounded by wherever there isn't white. She wants to go back there now. Gylan used to come sometimes and hold her where she hurt from his leaving.

Gylan drives past the Salvation Army at 96th on their way down Broadway to Fourth Street. Jane used to leave old clothes outside the building for the junkies and winos, who like an army of the living dead would surround the steps.

Uptown was Jane's off-and-on home. Tonight she has worn makeup for masquerade, bespeckling her eyelids and lips with golden glitter. She's left her pale skin translucent, not going for sheen or richness. There is only right and wrong, but they show up so differently in different places. Gylan had taught her things. Gylan's part of uptown, for example, still values chivalry. He had told her that without chivalry, there was no survival here. An individual life is an entire world populated by the significant and the vulgar and the tragic: no one dares touch it from the outside. He'd told her that she did not listen to him well enough, that she could not hear him.

Living a lot of different lives had been part of her plan. Her career. And finally something had changed her. It was the loss. He had become all she wanted. He had been her lover, her husband, her teacher. And he had said he wanted to leave. Nights she would shadow-dance in the glimmering radio light and whisper lyrics depicting the naturalness of their tableau. Their setting, which had become tyrant in her memory, had the intimacy of bed.

When she had met Gylan, he allowed her only a tenancy in his part of town. He stole her certainty and replaced it with doubt. Nothing was certain. Not the cement beneath her feet, nor even the practiced guile of her own face.

Gylan shapes his mouth around her earlobe and sticks his tongue deep into her. Still driving, he pulls his right hand out from between her thighs and draws her over to him. She gently pats her damp tawny hair falling in broken curls from her shoulders. Her dilated gray eyes moisten uncontrollably, gathering force. She disassociates from the pressure and floats. They have left uptown. Gylan parks his car and takes her to her door. He uses his key. The light of the moon, charmed by the objects it strikes as it enters the arched windows of Jane's Federal house, wobbles prisms across her red rug. Vine creepers crisscross the upper halves of the glass extending to the ceiling as frame to the cut-glass pitchers and bowls and drinking basins shelved across the window sill. Rich oakwood casements make furniture of the main floor windows so that they dominate the brick and plaster room. Jane believes that eventually the rawness and expectation of her life might cease, and in their place a deserved calm might lie restfully, periodically brushing her mind with the smooth shades of rhythm and routine. The rhythm should stop the waiting for something to happen, and the routine, the making something happen. Intimacy has a lot to do with forcing life to work, people make it their life's work. She had never wanted more than a series of single stationary events, posted in time, to accumulate in the place of living. When the events were completed, she could push them around like colorful acquisitions, and say they were she.

She had wagered that if she would go simply from one thing to the next, things that were daily—if she would eat a dinner, sleep a night through, wake in the morning and make coffee—perhaps she could stop the world from Picasso-ing her life.

The man looks like his eyes have been dipped in Hell. Her back is in the kitchen doorway so when he clutches for her right hand, she can still move a little further before she is against the wall. He looks at the back of her hand. Touches it. Feels the silver and gold band on her finger. She watches. He guides her hand down past his stomach and she pulls away.

"What are you doing? That's not happening."

"You know you're beautiful..."

"Yes."

She backs further into the kitchen and glances to her far right where the stainless-steel kitchen knives dangle on nails from the brick wall. He comes to her then, in one swift move, grabbing her buttocks and pulling her onto him, pressing himself into her. She laughs at first. She pushes his chest but he doesn't budge. His knees are bent and his balance is perfect.

He kisses her neck. She grabs the hair on the back of his head and yanks. His neck holds tight. He is very strong and trained. She has to concentrate. He is a monolith. The situation is absurd, but if she doesn't concentrate, her mind might slip and she could be in trouble. She might think she is some place else. The place that is white. Like a place that very long distance away. The fruit trees would be in bloom now and the blazing cardinals singing. There the scent of the trees is like that of cherry and orange, and the struggle to live is absent. She must concentrate.

He bends over in a hunch and holds her thighs. His fingers dig through her clothing and into her flesh. It hurts. She can't move her legs to kick. Only her arms are free, but his body is pressed so tightly against hers that she can't get between them to jab or push. She bites his neck. Hard. He tastes salty-sweet. He doesn't flinch. She bites so hard she expects to see blood gushing from his jugular vein, but he holds her, pushing his body into hers.

By pressing her arm against his back she works her sterling bracelet down her arm to her wrist and slams the side of it into his ear. Deadly intent prohibits his making a sound other than that of breath. She rakes her fingernails down his face and neck, still believing he won't force her. But he doesn't feel a thing.

"Please stop, talk to me for a minute. You don't mean to do this."

"You want me."

"Let's just talk a minute. Okay? Come on now, talk to me Gylan."

A peculiar odor hits her. It is metallic. At first she thinks of a gas leak. But it is coming from him. It smells like petroleum and rancid vegetables. His gray T-shirt feels dripping wet. He is in some other land working fiendishly away at her body. The smell makes him inhuman. It isn't natural. They are so close his sweat is hers. She kicks a leg free—in revulsion. The kitchen walls move a couple feet closer, oppressing her. She can see into her living room through the pass-through window on her kitchen wall. She wants to be sitting properly on her soft brown chair. From there she can look through the rich casement windows, out onto the perfect little cobblestone street lined with brownstones whose stillness reminds her of a Hollywood set.

She kicks free for a second and jabs her heel into the flesh of his left foot. He grabs for her leg so she slams her pelvic bone into his groin as hard as she can. He grabs her back to stop her thrust. She thinks she can stomp his foot again and lift her knee into his groin, but she can't reach him. He has too much control over her body. He presses a place in her hip and her leg won't rise more than an inch.

This is a terrible mistake. Her mind slips away a little. She doesn't let others in. If they want her, it has to be on her terms. She measures out time parsimoniously. She'd been a brass and guts girl, a drop-dead girl—until she had moved uptown and learned the games of the all night ramblers. Then her movements became careful, not too light, not too dark. Sometimes her expression taunted her own face. In the beginning with Gylan she would become excited, and out would slide a perfect design of words and sounds. Then she learned that when he said something like, *Chivalry is one of the armaments that balance reality*, she might trill with feeling, even epiphany, but she would show not one thing. The vibrance is gone now, yet there is sometimes a resonance. Like tonight, when she was playing.

Gylan has known her for 1,846 days and has seen her in person 936 of those.

She screams. He doesn't hear. Her mind slips a little. He kisses her neck. It is a gentle kiss. The highest crime. She must have looked at him straight on for a moment because he lets go of her back and grabs her face, forcing his mouth onto hers. She clenches her teeth. She will bite the tongue out of his head. Sensing her venom, he looks at her sad.

Her senses fade. The petroleum vapors deaden her nose. She begins to laugh uncontrollably. He shoves some fingers down the front of her black spandex skirt. In the distance somewhere he is madly pumping away at something, pushing hard. His silence sounds ghastly. He sweeps her legs out from under her and she crashes down hard against a box in the corner. As she falls her legs are pinned straight back underneath her. Gylan comes down on top of her strong, his arms and legs clamped around her body the way they had been so many times before, in moments of gentleness when the closeness was for dispelling any distance between them. Her legs cannot move. He'll break her neck before she can stop him. Jane can see the slight tremor of life moving through the bluish-green cords in his strong arms and hands.

The silky fur on his arms had picked up the color of the snow out the window, starting to descend into the pines in the distance with a wild intensity. It was the veins in Gylan's hands that added the extra vitality needed for that setting in white. Jane leaned into the palm of his fist as it unfolded from the shape of a red bird. She had stood up then and started to build a fire at the tremendous stone fireplace. He had walked up behind her and cupped her elbows in his hands, kissing her neck lightly, ever so slightly. He finished the fire as she watched his hands move deliberately and knowingly over the logs, their touch setting off the rippling in his forearms. She had felt a stirring in herself that increased as it came and went. But that was it. That was how it had begun, wasn't it?

He unzips his jeans. He jerks her hand down to touch him. His flesh is so familiar and tender. Soft like the air of the Caribbean sky. She knows him better than her own voice, her own hands. No contest with her own heart, so much so she cries. She leans down to him and takes him in her mouth, as she has done so many times. The hard within that vulnerability, which is the corner he has on human nature, is what she cannot get at, cannot touch.

She tears her nails into Gylan's tender flesh and with her other hand she brings the power of her fist down on his head. He is silent, but fierce. His shoulders shake suddenly. He shoves a hand back down the front of her underpants, against her stomach, and jams his finger deep up inside her. The thrust is endless. She stops breathing. His fingernail tears into soft flesh. He had always suspected that what she'd wanted for the past years was a death.

For what there had been uptown in the shade of the silver blinds, in the room of hard-backed books and soft penciled etchings, was for him a life. He sought that which followed wherever he was. Permanence in anything held no sway. He was capable of enduring things and being engaged by what he believed was beauty. He desired little. For her, it had been tenancy. She wanted to possess his life because it was the closest she could come to permanence. The imprecision of their fit drove her mad. The days that started out happiest she tore paintings from the wall, smashed pitchers filled with flowers he might have brought her against the stove or fireplace. What she couldn't accept was the uncertainty with him. In her relation to others, she had adapted. Before Gylan, she had always sought endings once something was begun, nothing in between was tolerable. And men could be used for that. Endings, that is.

Pain is not pressure unless there is a way out. A news commentator had said that. She is cornered. The distance between her head and the knife handle is only a few feet. Her knees are bent underneath her buttocks and the leg muscles are so cramped they might not work. She springs. Hard. And fast. She bangs her belly into the side of the oven with such force she knocks the wind out of herself.

All she can see is a gleam of steel in the distance. A straight flat white dancing thing. She grabs for it and turns. She cannot see him. She cannot hear him. She slashes out into the glow she's created. She wonders if he deserves to die but she doesn't feel a thing. She crouches down, crisscrossing her arms over her abdomen. Perhaps they will meet in a different club tomorrow and they will go home and make love like the old days. No anger. Leaning her head forward and waiting for the flush of blood that will bring back her eyesight, she feels a stirring under her left foot. It is Gylan. His hand. That exquisite hand she so loves. He grips her in a death hold.

"You cut up my side bad."

Gylan's voice sounds warm and familiar. There doesn't seem to be any blood that she can see.

"Where? Where did I get you?"

"Here."

As he points, blood starts to pump out.

"Lie over on your left side. Here, I'll help you."

"You won't let me die will you?"

"Of course not. I love you. Lie back and I'll take care of everything."

When she puts her arm under his body to lift him over she sees the knife still sticking in the back part of his waist. The laceration winds around his waist for about eight inches and the knife has lodged near his kidneys. She remembers swinging around him like a samurai killer.

She leans down and kisses his forehead. His eyes droop and a chill straightens her. She holds his head in her lap. She pulls off her blouse, wringing it horizontally and then flattening the underside. She places her hands on either side of the wound and pushes the opening together into a slit. Pressing the flesh as if the fingers of one hand were a butterfly bandage, she tries to pull the knife out of his body with the other hand. Letting go, she grabs the end of the knife with both hands and yanks. It won't give. She yanks again. It makes a slush sound as it slips out. Blood is everywhere. She throws the knife across the room and grips the pressure bandage she's made with her blouse. She presses the sides of the cut together again—it is cavernous—and leans down to pick up the bandage with her teeth, drops it on his body and then for a split second lets go of the cut with one hand, covers the opening with the makeshift bandage and then lays her body heavily on top of the wound to cause pressure.

"Come back to me baby," she croons, "wait just a minute."

He'll wait. Dying isn't his style. She thinks about the many things she has. She plucks sensation from the day breaking around them and fights to feel wired to their daily lives.

She had been beautiful. She called out in breezy animal voices when they made love. She'd traveled with him to learn uptown from downtown. Their fight contained structure. Honor was defined and prescribed. She could whisper about these things into the silence and it would shout back at her. Backatcha, she'd say, and throw the blues. She would turn on a song and ask Gylan to dance with her in the sunset light shooting through the window. She would dance asking him about the all night ramblers and he'd explain to her that all she needed to know he would tell her. Although she had not let anyone in before, and now she had embraced Gylan, she still had her ways. She'd moved uptown and learned the games of the all night ramblers even though he told her she didn't need to know. She already knew what she'd been nurtured to know. She'd wanted something more. Of that she had been certain. But when in search of something certain, she'd made her mistake. She'd gone beyond what Gylan wanted her to know.

Gylan had told her a fable when they first met. A boy had been exiled from his home, the village of his youth. Lack of faith, the aunts had said, was the cause. The boy thought it sad, but not unbearable. He had met up with a sardonic-eyed witty woman first and it was really she who had finally sent him to the old man. When he met the venerable old man who smoked *kif* and, like other *griots*, held the nuance of an entire civilization within the power of his mind, the boy moved to a beach tent where the fiery birds whispered thoughtlessly. The old man lived in the main house on this same beach. They were surrounded by water beasts. The old man taught the young man to wash his wooden floors with orange halves and to listen to the wail of the mountain women. They were fierce in a way the witty woman had not been. She had been *ça va*.

The old man told him it was said that no man could keep his mind if the river princess of the Atlas chose him as a lover. The time of year was usually autumn when the winds were passive and the spirits preoccupied with preparing their winter nests. The village women would begin their song faithfully, but with the regularity of illness the men would forget. They would return to the same riverbeds and complain about their women; how they did moan. The princess was not beautiful. Was not passionate. In the way a man thinks. She was compelling only because she *was*, and, more than anything, this was why their women hated her. She made lies of their lives and once every four seasons took one of their men. Brought him close to her thick waist and wrapped her legs covered with red down, the color of her special hair, around his head. No one knew what finally would happen. If she took a lover in the human way, or if her power lay in a unique sexual act.

The women saw the man after it was over, running through the streets of the village, his hair turned to copper wire, his eyes melted down to the size of roe, then multiplied so that thousands of tiny black nuggets filled the charred sockets that smelled with a vileness which forced the bearer of this stench to bleed from his nose and vomit from what was left of his mouth. The women stared, for he was their son or husband or father. The men looked away for they chose to forget. The body would be found by a stranger to the mountains and, out of fear, that stranger would burn the body into the air, or bury the body in the soil, or bind the body to a river rock deep in the water where after many months black river newts could be found.

Once, the old man had been that stranger. Before he buried the amphibious creature he opened up and inspected the body. It was as if it had been the receptacle for some other thing's sustenance, virtually acting as another's stomach until digestion was accomplished. The wind smelled of the fruit of the coriander plant, which bloomed only once a year, at the time of this victim's death. From these teachings the young man learned that the sardonic-eyed witty woman and his aunts were the ones who could understand him. He was a shadow of the rages running through his body. He should not have left the aunts of his village, or the woman who had sent him so close to the inviting river.

"So what is the moral, Gylan?" Jane had asked.

"Caution. Never be on the periphery of an event that is not your own. Home. The moral is about home," Gylan had said.

The night he knocks open the door to where she stands, she stands alone—the sun's first flame making of her a golden statue as she poses at that point equidistant from where her shadow, her image and the empty space declare themselves. He uses a .45 automatic with duck-stemmed bullets. The end is immediate. He is interested in honor, not torture.

In the years that follow he is not able to twist her face into focus, but at the glimpse of any dark, coil-haired, lanky manchild whose eyes have been dipped in Hell, he rushes to speak. He wants to make a gesture. He wants someone to know who he defended. *You've got to strike the mother sun if it strikes you*, he says.

THE COMPANY WE KEEP

TONIGHT DAVID HAS BROUGHT A GIRL to our house—we are spending the summer in adjacent cottages with David—and we all are going to dinner. David is Harry's best friend, the man I live with. However, I do not know David very well; he moved to California the year Harry and I got together. And that year I was not really with Harry anyway, because I was getting divorced and not really with anything. Now David is getting over a divorce. He was married to someone named Sarah, and she and David and Harry were a real threesome. I never met Sarah, but I've heard a lot about her—although she was David's wife, Harry carried a keen feeling for her around with him. David wishes it were a year from now. *Pain* is such a slight word. I don't want to tell him that a year is not long enough.

Anyway, here he is in our house with a girl half his age. He introduces her by saying their conversations duplicate those he has been having with his students. We cruise for an hour to a restaurant Harry knows will please David. David drives a big new silver Mercedes S600 he bought just before the divorce became final. Sarah left him.

The girl's name is Marisa. David and Harry address her as they speak but they quickly travel beyond what she could know. They are old friends and their timing is impeccable. Their humor has been nurtured in such a way that its vibrancy is fed by its own insulation. David puts a country rock-and-roll tape into his twelve-disk CD changer with a six-speaker sound system. Marisa has long slim legs, neither a crease nor a hair marring their symmetrical, sensual beauty. She knows this. There is a long slit up both sides of her dress, for maximum exposure.

None of her self-awareness—of her bronze legs, her graceful arms, her small, well-shaped breasts— is offensive to me. I luxuriate in it. She is young in the way I was young. She looks a little like my childhood friend Barbara Chatfield, although Barbara was short. I am now my mother's age when I first knew Barbara, but I knew those things about myself that

Marisa does, at her age. In fact, if the song happened to be a good one, each part of my body moved in its special way as if to join the music, accentuating whatever my magnetic appeal might have been, in the way Marisa is captivating us now. And at the same time I believed my nonchalance showed indifference to the attention I attracted, I wanted those eyes on me. I still do.

Harry pretends not to stare. He watches me watch, as if to say, You are betraying Sarah. Although I have been told that David's wife is lovely, one thing I can assume is that she does not have twenty-year-old legs that know the movement to each note of Rosanne Cash's last cut on the B side of her tenth album. I suspect that Sarah doesn't even know Johnny has a daughter named Rosanne who has put out ten albums. David knows, even though he used to listen only to Bach and the stars of *fado*. But the thing is, I am certain Sarah's eyes would be drawn to Marisa too. There is something to share among the three of us—in the way Marisa extends her arm across the back of David's headrest, in the way she lays her hand to rest on David's thigh. Sarah would recognize the gesture— not as her own, but as one that might be tried out in the company of others when those others are strangers and you are the exotic yet uneasy outsider. There is something to share, too, in the

way we, even Sarah and I, would always be out-
siders here.

Marisa is smart. Not intelligent. Harry has told
me that Sarah has intelligence. With her delicate
fingers, Marisa grabs for bread and applies too much
butter. I know that Sarah watches her weight, that
she is diminutive, but for very different reasons
would never put too much butter on her bread. She
is a gourmand. David and Harry and Sarah have
eaten all over the world together. And cooked. They
cooked the way New Yorkers who know about food
cook. Marisa twists her hand around so that the back
of it faces me, on the other side of the table, when
she eats. The style is not European. It is a simple
case of bad form. David doesn't notice. He talks
about his tan. Undoes the top buttons of his shirt
for Marisa to touch the soft hairs of his chest. Marisa
runs her slender fingers across the golden V David
has created by opening his shirt. I imagine Sarah
would have been compelled to do the same.

In part because of his physical beauty, David's
life is metaphor. David is a painter. He mixes hues
to paint a persimmon, using the color of his lips as
that from which he distills tone. A kiwi fruit in a
blue bowl might be the result of his wearing an aquamarine shirt the evening before painting. He loves
touch and poetry, wine and food, and attention.

David had always needed attending to in such a way that while providing it Sarah must have neglected to discover what it was she needed in return, blaming finally the marriage instead of herself for the omission. Why else could she have left in the way David told me she did. It was as if she had forgotten herself and, in her forgetting, there came into being a palpable absence between them that David filled in other ways. He cared about his fruit.

Harry winces. I look over to see Marisa caressing David. It is not the same as being witness to someone else's indiscretion, someone's affair. I understand what Harry is feeling. It is raw. It is knowing that Sarah will never again be to Harry's right and David's left as they sit to eat in Da Silvano or Provence in New York, or Al Moro in Rome, or drink in the wine bar where they all gathered during the five years Harry saw his shrink across the street from where Sarah worked.

The girl stares at another table, feigning distraction. David and Harry are discussing the wine. It is a '79 Antinori Solaia they brought to the restaurant and they are comparing its nose to the '82 Sassicaia they had at a friend's farther down the coast the night before. The Sassicaia tested out fruitier, the Solaia fleshier—but neither of these great Tuscan wines was at all suggestive of the fruit of the California reds. This is the dinner conversation, like so many others I have had with Harry, that follows the courses as smoothly as soft on suede. The girl knows California and Italian wines have come up in the world, so she says, but after a bounty of Taylor and Almaden for so many school years, she'd prefer a good nine-dollar Pouilly-Fuissé. French is her second language—three years' worth. David and Harry exchange glances. Harry is a translator by trade, a poet and novelist by heart. As an upstart newcomer to the literary and second-son social world of an earlier Tangier, he wrote an original and very avant-garde novella in ancient Greek under the name Javert and then translated it for publication in *The Kenyon Review* under his own name. He was criticized for the arrogance of his debut, but it acknowledged the arrival of a presence.

When the soup arrives, the girl has already consumed five pieces of bread. David and Harry move smoothly from wine to food. David starts:

"What's in this? There's something unusual here. It's not just halibut and eggplant. I think they put in walnuts and basil. Sarah would know."

"It's not walnuts," says Marisa. "There aren't any nuts in this soup, David!"

Determined to be heard, Marisa knows that David's wife is a food person. Just as she has spoken, however, her teeth hit something hard.

"Could be eel eggs ground up a little." Harry's grin is grim. He feels uncomfortable. The conversation is both reminiscent and lacking.

I don't say anything. The hardest thing I have bitten into is a radish. But if Sarah were here, I am sure the conversation would go on for another five minutes until the chef was called from the kitchen and the mystery solved. I scrutinize Marisa. She is beginning to notice her lack of function here. Smart girl.

Marisa is full. She has had too much bread. She takes an aggressive stance. "I can't finish this soup. It's too rich and too much. They should have put it in smaller bowls."

David agrees with her and slips his hand through her short-cropped hair. The Polaroids I have seen of Sarah show her off as a small, pretty woman with short hair. Marisa's hair is short like Sarah's, but thicker. I wonder as David touches the hair if he thinks for a moment he has recaptured the naturalness of brushing through his wife's hair. He lingers with Marisa. He listens to her.

Only this morning he said—simply, and without preface, as we three sat on the beach reading— "Sarah doesn't love me anymore." Harry put his book down and didn't speak. I didn't have to say anything. I had not been a part of their trio. Yet I hurt for David. I am touched by the fact that he still thinks in terms of love. Sarah hadn't even called to find out if he was doing all right, although the week before he arrived at our doorstep they had divided all their worldly possessions and said good-bye for the last time. An amicable divorce. That is what Sarah's guilt would call it, I suppose. I looked at the two men as I began to recall the ache David must feel, remembering the vivid physical quality of it. After a silence, it was David who spoke first. He asked me if I thought his legs were as tan as mine. I said we had different kinds of skin. He said his legs are always the last thing on his body to tan.

I am not sure how good Harry and I are. We have become pleasingly packaged. We Cuisinart our way through the weekends, trim city plants and window herb gardens, buy important California wines and still lifes, have chosen psychiatrists over psychologists and listen to jazz on a stereo system made by some computer whiz kids in LA, instead of being there live in a club or after-hours jam joint like Mikell's. I used to hear about this kind of life; I even had contact with some old college friends who lived it. But I wasn't interested in circumscribed living back in the days when I'd hit Mikell's and boogie into the early morning dancing hours, when the day would resolve itself in ecstasy, mind fighting or miscellaneous horror. There is a terrifying undertow all around me now, but with great delicacy Harry and I skip around it, avoiding it with appetites for subtlety and stories in translation. I for reasons of survival, Harry for entirely logical reasons. He would rather smoke tuna in foil over a wok filled with tea leaves than discuss why he walked out on me the first month we were together, only to return two days later. Perhaps it was because, although my past wasn't easy for him to comprehend, I never hurt anybody. Impressed on my life there's a value which Harry intuited.

One morning before I left for work, Harry called me over to where he was sitting—at his desk, as every morning—with his books and his strong Italian brewed coffee. He keeps a journal of quotations and snippets, which includes everything from a picture of Calvino in the forties when he styled his hair after Dick Powell for a photo session, to cutouts of camels or favorite *non sequiturs* of former lovers. That particular morning it was a quotation from one of Updike's books. There was a woman who, when she stepped out onto a brisk New England coastal dock from the warmth of the cozy diner where she'd eaten lunch, was struck by the beauty and power of the winter as it changed the color of the water to a steelier blue and the clapboard houses to a more startlingly white white, "every nail hole vivid." Harry read to me what this woman thought at exactly that moment and how she "felt frightened that her own beauty and vitality would not always be part of it, that someday she would be gone like a lost odd-shaped piece from the center of a picture puzzle." I hadn't slept the night before, and Harry had tossed and turned with my absence from our bed. I said I lived every day like the woman lived that one moment, and Harry took the journal gingerly from my hands, gripped me tightly in his embrace and explained how it was not for the everyday—that feeling. Harry loves Morandi and irony and pleasure; I spent one year in prison after being caught for an act I believed was a call to duty, then some more time with a lefty militant cell as company, trying to find where I might fit, once the puzzle had changed and my husband had walked. Harry is with me for my passion, I with him for his constancy, not to me but to enthusiasm; and I must wait for one of his delicately circumscribed poems or stories to discover, in retrospect, his experience of me.

David is talking to Marisa and Harry about his life. His yearning is voracious. He wants everything, which is what?—everything, he says, as much as I can get of what there is. He will be fifty soon. He is making plans for the next year, the next month, the next week, and Marisa is wondering if she will be a part of any of these plans. However, what Marisa doesn't realize yet is that she has already vaporized for the moment. David and Harry are on a run now. Talking in that very intimate inside-chat language of artists speaking about great artists now past. Harry pushes David's ego. The crescendo is terrific. Their brilliance is breathtaking. When Wright was in Yugo at Lake Ohrid, he finally surrendered entirely to the dark-eyed beauty with the long knife scar down the inside of her arm. Her mother was a gypsy from the Croatian lands. And it was the gypsy in her that made it possible for the mermaids of the lake to appear naturally later in the song. The song was unrhymed quatrains, predictably syllabic.

Marisa listens in rapt attention. Sarah probably would have as well, although I hear that sometimes she would quickly slip in a comment here or there if the boys stopped to catch their breath.

They discuss the poets—Lowell, Berryman and Schwartz—their lives and work, the summer they all spent congregating in Damariscotta, just up the coast from where we are now summering, and then their deaths. But mostly they speak intimately of how their favorite lines of each poet explain the stark insanity these men endured—pain similar to their own (but of course not their own, they'd never let those individual pains loose)—the torture of creation, not conceivable to the uninitiated. Harry quotes

Berryman, who wrote about a night in Maine when he doffed his clothes and took off across the damp grass and nearby bluff that led to the water—this cold, turgid northern Atlantic water that he intended to walk beneath forever. Marisa has never heard of Berryman. She'd been an Econ major and the idea of some man imagining himself walking underwater instead of on the surface seems unproductive to her. She says so, but the boys don't notice.

I stand up and excuse myself. They don't notice. Neither David nor Harry has been jailed or institutionalized for madness, or jumped off a bridge into a frozen Mississippi River. It is unlikely they will enter the madness that was Schwartz's and be found dead in a welfare hotel. They've never had to smooth their moods with a palliative any stronger than Valium or wine. I believe these two know torment, but I believe they react to their fear of it in ways the initiated should not. If they are the analysts of human tumult, they should not flee from where shadows go in the dark. Yet the poems they speak of are self-referential, the discussion is indifferent to reality, aloof to its real horror and grandeur, and to the act of bearing witness to such as strange fruit. The conversation can only make people who are not a part of it feel uninitiated. And of course, that is part of its purpose—and for that reason more than any other, I understand why Sarah finally left.

As I stand in front of the mirror in the ladies' room, I know that I would like to be Marisa tonight, expectant of new passion; my long legs, although twenty years older, are able to move with a suppleness I feel can still compete with anyone. I will be forty in another year. At this age my mother was watching me grow into a twelve-year-old with dark-rimmed eyes and a friend with ratted hair—Barbara Chatfield. We used to tease our hair together in the bathroom that had built-in double sinks for me and my sister. Ratted hair, we called it. We would rat our hair into high peaks of fine flaxen hives. My mother used to try to add some class by calling the procedure back-combing, but finally she gave up and simply forbade me to rat my hair.

One night Barbara and I were getting ready to go to the football game at North High School, which was not in our district. The bad kids were at North. The hoods. My mother had told me I couldn't go. I usually did what she said, but it seemed like such an unreasonable prohibition on her part that I told her I was going anyway. I was twelve and Barbara was twelve too and we were in junior high school together. I had just moved to Kansas City and was still in public school, where the girls put black eyeliner around their eyes, even on the inside lip of the rim. Both on the top and on the bottom. And that night, in total defiance of my mother, I stood with

Barbara, each of us in front of a sink, and ratted first my hair and then Barbara's short hair. Hers was mostly on top of her head. The sides had been cut short. So with the teasing, she had this big high head and tiny little body. Then we applied our eyeliner. My sister was already away at a girls' school studying music, and the last time she had been home and seen my ratted hair she had called me a slut. I had never done anything but put black eyeliner on my rims and tease my hair, and here I was a slut. When my mother joined in to call me a slut the night of the North football game, that did it. I was never to do anything girl-type naughty again, but I certainly did everything else, including bomb an empty government building and end up on the lam for six months. But no slut stuff.

Something tugs my mind as I lean into the friendly bathroom lights while Harry waits at the table. Barbara had wide brown eyes, as if there could be a field of brown heather between the lashes. I wonder what she is going through now—now that we are about to become our mothers' age. Has she been divorced as I have? Is she without a child yet and therefore more of a child herself than our mothers before us at the same age? I still listen to Diana Ross and the Temptations, Eddie Kendricks singing about imagination more vividly than any bard. In front of the stereo, or with my headphones on, as loud as the ear can hear, I dance for hours in the dark, where fantasies come to life. I feel my strength when I dance, like the strength we had as children. That terrible hardness that promises us immortality. Even when we think we know about death, our conviction is that it is endless. That it is all possible. There is plenty of it all to go around. Time is what I'm thinking about— and friendships, as with Barbara. Relationships, like David and Sarah's. The big things. And now—now I don't feel that way. Does Barbara? Do her years have boundaries, specific memories associated with a unit of time, each one unique? I knew exactly when I had a particular thing, what it felt like. And which of those things I have since lost. Which are likely to be regained and which others are not. I feel my strength return when I dance. Always before, when there was the inevitability of change, no matter how sad, it was encompassed by the blind knowledge of youthfulness. For the first time that knowledge does not keep me company. I am a child at living without it, without the sureness of being young. All the hard child promises are leaving. On the other hand, neither are so many things irrevocable—abrupt—as they once seemed. Thoughts of return and certainty give an uneasy comfort as I dance now.

Youth is no loss to David tonight. I respect him for that. His energy has great resonance. He is the purist tonight. I leave the ladies' room revved.

I walk back to the table where Marisa is looking about angrily. Marisa, whose sensual antennae were so attuned to David only moments ago that the barest touch held an eroticism beyond any sexual act, rebukes David now when he reaches out to her as he continues speaking to Harry. The iridescence of David's jade-blue shirt is stunning as it hits his tanned skin. With his fascinating gift for articulating beauty, he carefully describes to Harry why he has placed the Italian peasant pitcher in the foreground of his new painting. Its whiteness will dominate, and while David articulates the significance of this, I am thinking that with his precise mind and his own terrific beauty, it is quite possible that David himself approaches that abstract notion of human perfection. Harry absently taps the fingers of my hand holding the stem of the red-wine glass. Marisa looks from one of the men to the other and slowly, individually, grips each with an eye of contempt. She is supposed to be central to this evening. In the midst of David's explanation, Marisa interrupts. She says that she was not an Econ major for nothing. She emphasizes the word *nothing*, and comprehends the effect of the words she has used to make the comment. She is interested not simply in the economy of lands and their finance, but of abuse, of feelings, of language. It is because of people like us she has found value in economizing. We who

manufacture gratuitous pain, exert effort in under-
takings such as walking underwater. We mourn too
long and speak too much. We substitute talk for
sex and food for eating. Marisa is playing her hole
card, testing David, who finally turns to her. Harry
leans back in his chair, bored with Marisa's out-
burst. He hates to see David interrupted.

I point to a man as he leaves the restaurant. Harry
sees what I mean. The man is dressed in a suit, but
bulging from every pocket, including the breast, are
the articles of his daily commerce—pencils, pads, a
tool used for computers, handkerchiefs, stray strings,
paper clips and rubber bands. Harry asks first—
Which is his? Outside the restaurant a line of cars is
parked on the quaint little street. I point to a blue
sedan, perfectly presentable at first glance but upon
inspection filled with the odds and ends of a life—
screwdrivers, a shirt, books, newspapers, even a
bottle of wine. The man steps out of the restaurant
and hesitates on the doorstep, looking up the street
and down, enjoying the azure beginnings of sunset
on the port, struck perhaps by the beauty and power
of the summer sea, each docked fishing boat vivid
against the darkening water. We wait until he lei-
surely strolls to the blue sedan. Then Harry and I
touch pinkies as the entree is served and the tender
pink meat of the fresh salmon in its intense green
sorrel sauce becomes the topic of conversation.

The ocean, pinned alongside the road we travel back to our little vacation village, is stippled with moonbeams. It is as if the turbulence of the water lifts the waves up to the refulgent night light so that the sea will shimmer. Large shelves of driftwood become flotsam in the dark air and the slate and its rockweed appear as pirates of a modern sort, with long flowing hair and arm bands. Harry tries to take my hand. I pull it away. His hair shapes a friendly halo around his face and I wish it could always look just as it does now. His father died when he was very young, so endings to him came early. Since then he has refused to start anything, until he met me.

Though there is, between us, a humor, we are tentative. Once when we were in Rome, where Harry says there are more priests than flies, I was suddenly petulant and quiet. I couldn't explain to him why. Well, he said, once I was quiet, but I went to see some people who lived on a soft carpet and I twirled into the middle of their favorite color and danced so well I was offered a Hollywood contract, which I turned down because of my impending ambassadorship to Jodrellia. And on and on he went.

The heat of the evening is waning and now I think of Harry and our summer bed, surrounded by windows which look out onto water and sky. Exactly where the elements meet is sometimes not at first apparent. There is no land, no shard of stone even, to break their contiguity. We float at night in the unseasonable chill of the strip of land that is so far from our city home. This morning, when the sun did not come up over the sea and neither the night dampness nor the thick grayness out our window was broken, I looked to Harry's sleeping face for definition. I take his hand now in the back seat of David's silver Mercedes, tighten the grip of his fingers resting against the soft leather of the car's interior—and so thank him for his company.

ABOUT THE AUTHOR

JEANNE WILMOT is a former Manhattan attorney who now lives in Princeton, New Jersey with her husband and their daughter, Lily. Her work has appeared in numerous magazines, and has been included in *The O. Henry Awards.*